a Mí

Will (ry) in

The Courage to Choose

Adapted by KATE EGAN

D0315651

HarperCollins *Children's Books*

This book was first published in the USA in 2004 by Volo/Hyperion Books for Children
First published in Great Britain in 2006 by HarperCollins *Children's Books*, a division of
HarperCollins Publishers Ltd.

© 2006 Disney Enterprises, Inc.

ISBN 0-00-720951-7
ISBN13 978-0-00-720951-4

1 3 5 7 9 10 8 6 4 2

The HarperCollins website is:
www.harpercollinschildrensbooks.co.uk

Visit www.clubwitch.co.uk

Printed and bound in Italy

ONE

Hay Lin stood in the lobby of Cornelia's apartment building, clutching the purple bag that hung from her shoulder. It felt good to have something to squeeze. At that moment, she had no clue what to do.

Hay Lin and Taranee were waiting for Irma, who was just stepping out of the elevator. She barely glanced in their direction as the doors closed. Instead, she tromped down the short marble staircase that led to the front door of the building. The stairs were covered in plush pink carpeting, and Irma was wearing delicate sandals that tied around her ankles like toe shoes, but Hay Lin could still hear the pounding of Irma's feet. Irma was that mad.

"Come on, Irma! Don't be like that!

Wait!" Hay Lin called as Irma rushed past her.

Irma's mouth was turned down firmly at the corners. "No!" she growled. "We came here to talk, and we got a door slammed in our faces. As far as I'm concerned, there's nothing more to say. And this time, I mean it!"

Catching Taranee's eye as Irma stormed away, Hay Lin could tell that Taranee looked worried. Taranee never liked it when Irma went off on a rampage.

Classic Irma, Hay Lin thought as she followed her outside. The water girl had a tendency to go from boiling mad to ice cold. Wonder how long we'll have to wait for her to thaw out.

The building's doorman was watering flowers beside the large front door. As Irma slammed it open, he touched his hat politely and said, "See you, miss!"

She didn't bother to be polite. "Don't count on it," Irma muttered.

"You won't solve anything by walking away like this!" Taranee yelled at Irma's back.

"Guess again!" Irma replied, waving her hand in the air dismissively. "I'd bend over backward for a friend, but I'm not going to let somebody treat me like this, especially when I'm trying to help her. You don't know me very well, Taranee."

Ouch, thought Hay Lin. It was true Taranee hadn't known Irma for very long. But they'd been through a lot together. For one thing, they'd saved the world. . . .

It seemed like just yesterday that Hay Lin and Taranee – along with Cornelia, Irma, and their friend Will – had been transformed from ordinary students at the Sheffield Institute into Guardians of the Veil. What did that mean? Oh, just that they were the five people chosen to keep the world safe.

Long ago, the beings in Candracar, an ethereal world that existed somewhere between space and infinity, had created the Veil, to protect the earth from a dark and dangerous ruler in a place called Metamoor. The Veil had endured, but it had begun to come apart when the new millennium rolled around. Openings in the Veil had to be repaired, so that the world could be safe. It was a job for the five Guardians of the Veil!

And where were the openings in the Veil? The portals just happened to be in Hay Lin's hometown, Heatherfield. So that they could do the job, the girls were granted some major magic powers over each of the elements.

Suddenly, Hay Lin was able to fly! Her power was over the air – with it she could fly like a bird and lift objects with her own personal gusts of wind. Irma's power was over all things watery, from puddles to oceans. Taranee could conjure up fire. Cornelia was all about the earth. And Will's power was the most mysterious of all. She was the Keeper of the Heart of Candracar, an iridescent pink orb, nestled in a magnificent silver clasp, that popped into her palm whenever she needed it. While the girls could morph into Guardian form without the Heart, they were more powerful when the Heart was present. The girls changed into bigger, better versions of themselves. They were superstrong and superglam – they even had wings! And when Will brought the girls' powers together using the Heart, the five were unstoppable.

So, naturally, peace in Metamoor had been restored, and the rightful queen returned to the throne. The mission had been accomplished. And, with the Oracle's help, the open portals had been closed and sealed.

Then, everything had gone downhill.

First, Cornelia had dropped out of sight. Hers was a tragic story. Prince Phobos was a bad guy they'd fought in Metamoor, and an evil man. The cunning prince had turned Cornelia's love, Caleb, a rebel leader in Metamoor, into a flower. Now Cornelia stayed holed up in her bedroom, tending to Caleb's leaves and watering his soil. Nobody could even get close to her – let alone talk to her.

Then, suddenly, it wasn't just Cornelia who was keeping her distance. The girls just didn't get along the way they had before.

Small disagreements blew up into major arguments. Tensions were at an all-time high. And that wasn't all. Just as Cornelia vanished, and just as the friends started fighting, their powers started to weaken. It happened slowly at first. One girl's power would disappear here, another's there. The magic was hard to control, but at least it was around. Then . . . nothing.

Which came first? Hay Lin wondered. Did the fighting start because our magic was gone? Or did the magic stop because we were fighting? All I know is that I feel like my wings have been clipped since our powers went AWOL. I'd do almost anything for the carefree feeling of floating on air again. Now, sometimes, I just don't feel like dealing with everyone, Hay Lin thought. There is too much drama.

Then something huge had happened. Will's mum had decided she wanted her company to transfer her out of Heatherfield. She and Will had been fighting, too, and Will's mum thought that maybe she and Will could use a change of scenery. She had no idea about W.I.T.C.H., which is what the girls called their group. (The first letters of their names – Will, Irma, Taranee, Cornelia, and Hay Lin – spelled the word.) She had no idea what she was doing to her daughter.

Even though they were bickering, the girls knew they couldn't let Will move away. It was their job to stick together. And together, maybe, they thought, they could work enough magic to obtain Will's mother's resignation letter and prevent it from being submitted.

Hay Lin thought about what had happened at Simultech.

With Will, Irma, Taranee, and Hay Lin went downtown to Simultech where Will's mum worked, because they were pretty sure the letter was in a safe in her boss's office. Will managed to unite the four powers even without Cornelia, and the girls blasted a major hole in the wall.

Everything seemed ok . . . until Will noticed a blue blob staring out of the hole in the wall. The blob shifted shape and took on the aspect of each of the girls in turn. Then it jumped out the window and ran toward downtown! Soon they figured out that, for some reason, the blob was trying to meet Cornelia.

Someone had the bright idea to warn Cornelia that a shifty energy blob might be on her tail. Hay Lin headed with Taranee and Irma toward Cornelia's luxurious penthouse apartment. They were too late, though. The blob took the form of Will – and Cornelia hugged it! Then the blob vanished, and Cornelia passed out on the floor. When she came to, Irma had to go and tease her. Hay Lin didn't really blame Cornelia for throwing them out.

Now we're right back where we started, Hay Lin thought. No magic. No peace.

"You shouldn't judge Cornelia!" Taranee

scolded Irma as they stood outside the Hales' apartment building. "She's not the same old Cornelia who will joke around with you."

"Nope! She's worse than ever!" Irma spat. "I'm done!"

Hay Lin watched Irma rant. She knew that when she got like that, Irma was too stubborn to be reasoned with.

Maybe, thought Hay Lin, if I ignore it, this tantrum will pass. But a voice in the back of her mind kept nagging. What if Irma had gone too far this time? What if she and Cornelia really were "done"?

"I'm sure what happened between Cornelia and that creature must have freaked her out," Hay Lin said. "It must have been a very strange meeting for her."

Irma wheeled around, crossed her arms over her chest, and rolled her eyes. "Oh, please!" she said sarcastically. "She was already strange before."

Irma and Cornelia had always sparred. Even though they were good friends, they were very different. And often they fought like sisters, pushing each other's buttons. Irma was all about fun. She was a flirt who loved being the centre of attention. Cornelia, on the other hand, was cool and collected – sort of a control freak. She had a hard time being patient with anyone, and didn't always share Irma's sense of humour.

"I ran into that pudding-faced chameleon, too, and I didn't go out of my head!" Irma continued to lament. "We've been up against worse things!" She pounded her fist into her open palm. "Cornelia has no excuse for behaving like that. She kicked us out – *that's* what gets me!"

Hay Lin sighed. It was true that Cornelia had kicked them out and slammed the door, but to be fair, Irma had needled Cornelia about Caleb. No wonder Cornelia had lost it!

"Irma, Cornelia wouldn't have done it if you hadn't . . ." she tried to say.

"Give me a break, Hay Lin!" Irma said, cutting her off. "You should stop trying to make excuses for her."

Hay Lin looked at the ground, frustrated. If I can't get through to Irma, who can? she wondered.

"See you guys," Irma said as she stalked away.

Confrontation wasn't Hay Lin's thing.

It wasn't Taranee's thing, either, come to think of it. But Taranee was standing there glaring over the tops of her glasses in a way that meant serious business.

While Taranee was the most tentative of the Guardians and had to think and think before taking action, she looked pretty sure of herself at that moment. These days, Taranee's fiery powers probably couldn't even have ignited a match, but that didn't matter at the moment. The girl was on fire!

"Go ahead and leave," Taranee shouted.

Irma turned back to glare at Taranee.

Pushing her glasses up on the bridge of her nose, Taranee switched to a calmer and more reasonable tone. "Think it over, Irma. Cornelia's our friend. We have to stick together."

"You do what you want!" Irma replied. She wasn't giving any ground. "I certainly won't be the one to stop you. But this time, count me out!" She marched off down the street without another word.

Hay Lin watched her pass a phone booth, round the corner, and disappear. She tapped her thin fingers nervously on the top of her bag. So that's it, she thought. Three down, two to go.

She adjusted the goggles she liked to wear on top of her head. They kept her shiny black hair in place – and they made quite the funky fashion statement. "Now what do we do?" she asked Taranee.

Looking her straight in the eye, Taranee seemed imbued with a renewed sense of purpose. "Whatever we do, we can't just sit around waiting!" she said firmly. "We've got to get Will. Try to get her mum to let her leave the house tonight. Make something up. . . . Beg. . . . Do anything!"

March into Will's house and interrupt the mother of all fights? The one that was determining Will's fate this very second? Uh-uh, Hay Lin thought, I don't like the way that sounds.

But just then, Taranee was as convincing as a lawyer at the end of a trial. Taranee's mum was a judge, so maybe she'd picked up a few tips on persuading people even when they had plenty of reasonable doubts.

"The important thing is for you to bring Will here!" Taranee continued.

Hay Lin nodded. She totally agreed. "Ok. And you? What's your plan?" she asked.

As Taranee looked up at the sky, the bright orange sun glinted in her glasses like one of the tremendous flames she had used to shoot at bad guys. She clenched her fists and exclaimed, "I'm going back to Cornelia's to find some way to make her open that door and talk to me!"

TWO

Cornelia knelt on the floor in the middle of her living room, gazing at Caleb in his flower form with a concentration so intense that she was not aware of anything else: neither the rustling of the curtains in the window nor the sun beginning to go down in the distance nor the baleful stare of the cat, Napoleon, who observed her from one corner of the room. All she could see or think about was Caleb.

Wrapping her hands lovingly around the antique vase where her precious flower grew, she inhaled the sweet scent and sighed. Tears welled up in her eyes.

I should be used to this by now, Cornelia thought. This feeling is nothing new.

But the tears stung as sharply as they had the first time they'd come, moments after her Caleb had been so cruelly transformed. I will *never* get used to this, she admitted to herself. Why, oh, why, did this have to happen?

A familiar despair washed over Cornelia as she considered that question for what seemed the billionth time. She bent her head; her forehead touched Caleb's tallest petal.

Does he know what I'm thinking? she wondered. If only he understood how I treasure every moment we spent together.

Cornelia willed Caleb to hear her thoughts, to see the images that were played and replayed on a relentless loop in her mind: his hand in hers; his strong arms wrapped around her and the magical kisses; his brave leadership of the Metamoorian rebels; his triumphant overthrow of Prince Phobos; his terrible face-off with the darkest of dark forces . . .

Now the tears flooded down Cornelia's face, blinding her to everything but the image of her lost love. I have to face it, she thought. He is gone. Or, rather, he is here but not here, mine but not mine, and it's hard to keep hope alive against the odds. It's so frustrating! After all, I can reach deep into the earth to call upon the power in all living things, but the power to change this one small flower back into Caleb may never be mine. What good is it to have all this power . . . and not be able to use it?

Power . . . magic . . . Suddenly another image flashed into Cornelia's mind: the image of her friends, at the height of their powers, working together to defeat Phobos's slimy henchmen. Cornelia remembered happily. Then, she saw the image of her friends at her door, telling her something she did not want to hear.

Cornelia could still see the disbelief on their faces as she turned from them. She could still hear the heavy slam of her door and feel their disappointment. But it seemed as if it had all happened a lifetime ago, instead of mere minutes before. All that mattered now was Caleb.

As she looked up, Cornelia scanned the room. Her family was out at the movies, so she was alone in the apartment, except for the watchful Napoleon, who was quietly curled up in a corner by the window. Cornelia felt utterly alone, as usual. But she also felt different from the way she usually felt.

What is it? she wondered. I feel sad, but I also feel strong: stronger than I have in a long time.

Now that she'd figured it out, Cornelia reflected on her power. She thought of the way the trees and plants must feel during the spring, when new leaves sprouted and flowers bloomed. That was how she felt, Cornelia realised.

Cornelia's heart was beating very fast.

It's as if I'd just finished a marathon without getting out of breath, she thought. It's the way I felt when I first saw Caleb, or the moment when he first kissed me. It's the same feeling I got when the power to control the earth was at my fingertips. The feeling was as if all these things were happening all at once!

For the first time in a long while, Cornelia was happy.

Suddenly, a blissful vision came to her. She stood up and stretched and then returned her gaze to the flower in the vase. What if Caleb really can hear me? she thought. Gently, she touched one of the petals of the lily. What if she could transform him? Her heart raced even faster at the thought of that possibility. She felt powerful and unstoppable. The feeling was so wonderful that Cornelia shouted at the top of her lungs. "I don't know how or why," she said, "but I have the feeling I can do it!"

Closing her eyes, she drew her fist to her chest. "I have the feeling I can't get it wrong!" she cried. "Caleb, I'll bring you back to life!"

Fear flashed through Cornelia's mind for a moment, but she banished it immediately. She could see magic in the room, great shafts of brilliant green light swirling around her like a hurricane. *I only have to make the magic do my bidding!* she thought.

With power coursing through her, Cornelia conjured up two large streams of energy and hurled them through the air at Caleb, who suddenly seemed very small and extremely fragile in his delicate vase.

My magic will protect him, she thought, full of confidence. *Yes, my magic will rescue him from the terrible spell!*

With all of her might, Cornelia thrust the magic energy toward the small, potted flower, the centre of her universe.

Whoooosh!

The magic bounced right back into

Cornelia's face. It was as if she had thrown a rubber ball at a wall. Cornelia looked wildly around the room trying to figure out what had happened.

What did I do wrong? she wondered. How can it be? How can this power defy me?

It wasn't until she looked down that Cornelia realised that everything had gone exactly according to plan. She'd been transformed! Now she had the flowing blonde hair and the longer legs of her magical self. She was wearing a long pink skirt and a blue top that clung to her new curves. Her wings were small and pointed. They fluttered in anticipation of whatever would come next.

It's the first step toward using any Guardian magic! Cornelia thought, rejoicing. But, she realised, I'm without my friends, the other Guardians. I'm on my own this time. The power is all mine.

For a moment, Cornelia felt the full force of her grief. She missed the Power of Five and being part of W.I.T.C.H. Why did I push the girls away? she wondered.

Once again, however, she struggled for control of the situation. She was sterner with herself than she'd ever been.

"No! I – I can't – I won't break down right now!" she yelled, so that Caleb would know it, too. "I will wrestle this magic until it obeys my command. There is only one possible outcome – the outcome of my dreams!"

Again and again Cornelia tried to channel the magic toward Caleb; but the energy kept slipping from her fingers.

This magic is awesome, she thought after a while. There is no other way to describe it. The power seems stronger than it's ever been before. But it's also harder to handle.

Cornelia vowed not to let the power intimidate her – after all, she had worked magic under adverse conditions many times before. It was all part of the job given to her and the others by the Oracle.

Try as she might, though, Cornelia could not get the magic under control.

I don't like this, she fumed. This is not working.

Cornelia still felt a massive surge of power, but she also felt discouraged. She lay down on the floor to snuggle next to Caleb as best she could. She wanted to be close to him.

The magic is so strong that I can't keep up with it, she thought. How I wish I had someone to talk to! My friends are out of the question now. . . .

But Cornelia squashed that thought as soon as it appeared in her mind. It doesn't matter, she thought, if I can confide in my friends – I can confide in Caleb!

Drawing closer to Caleb's vase, she whispered sadly, "It's all so difficult! I've tried everything I can think of to fix things, but nothing's happened. I don't know what to do anymore!"

Then, she thought, I sound pathetic. Horrible. Selfish. He doesn't need this from me. Caleb must not worry!

Cornelia lifted her eyes and pounded her hand on the floor. "I've never felt so powerful! There's a new strength inside of me!" she announced defiantly.

Cornelia took one of Caleb's petals between her hands. "I'm not going to give up!" she told him. "It won't end like this, Caleb! You'll come back, and we'll be together again!" She was sure that his leaves perked up at the sound of her words.

Caleb had remained strong through even

his harshest trials. At one time he'd been a Murmurer, a powerless flower inside the wicked court of Prince Phobos. Some Murmurers acted as spies for the Prince, but not her Caleb. He had taken on a human form. Then he had organised the resistance, and toppled Phobos at last!

"Your own force of will changed you from a Murmurer into a warrior!" Cornelia cried. "I have a strong will, too. I can do this.

"Oh, how could Phobos have so cruelly turned you into a flower?" she added. Just thinking about it revved her up, revived her. She wasn't about to give up without a fight. Caleb was her true love – they were meant to be together. "My power will give you back to yourself!" she promised Caleb. She was ready to get back to work!

But as Cornelia turned away from her flower, a strange thing happened. The curtains in the window flapped like sails in a squall. Then there was a voice in the distance, deep and serious.

"Stop, Guardian!" the voice ordered. "Do not break the age-old rules of Candracar!"

"What's going on?" Cornelia snapped.

"Who's there? Who said that?" She felt a little scared.

Her questions were met by an icy silence. And suddenly, Cornelia felt more furious than afraid.

I cannot . . . I must not be interrupted now! she thought. I must not waste a single second or a scrap of my power! This is no time to go all weak and act like a scaredy-cat.

"Come out and face me!" Cornelia demanded. "Who are you?"

In response, the curtains billowed. There was a puff of smoke in the window and a chilly breeze. Then a figure appeared, wearing flowing white robes and holding a glittering blue staff. So that was the source of the voice, Cornelia thought. "If you need to see me, child," it rumbled, "then take a good look!"

Cornelia was astonished by the sound of the icy voice. She could hardly think straight. "I – I know you!" she stammered. "I saw you once in Candracar!"

She'd seen that figure standing beside the Oracle, the benevolent and all-knowing being who ruled over Candracar. The Oracle emanated light and kindness. This figure . . . this creature . . . whatever it was . . . did not. It had the face of a cat, with long, scraggly whiskers and a wet black nose. It had long pointy ears and the body of a woman. Her mouth was equal parts human and feline and was twisted into a snarl, exposing two rows of little teeth.

"I am Luba, Keeper of the Aurameres. . . ." the cat-woman announced. "And I order you to stop!"

Rage flooded through Cornelia's body and soul. How dare this woman stand between me and my magic? she thought. Between me and my love?

"What you are trying to do is forbidden by the laws of Candracar!" Luba droned.

I don't care if my magic is forbidden by the Oracle himself, Cornelia seethed. I will not be stopped. "You're wasting your time," she informed Luba.

Luba pursed her cat lips disapprovingly. "Your power is as great as your insolence, little girl!"

Am I losing momentum? What is going on? Are my powers fading? I must return to Caleb at once! Cornelia thought, distressed. Losing this chance would be like losing him all over again.

And that I can't – I won't!—abide.

Cornelia remembered the pain of the moment when the real Caleb had disappeared. She remembered the agony of the weeks since she had seen him last in his human form. She could still taste the tears that she had cried for her lost love. I will not let it happen again, she promised herself.

Then, like a volcano, Cornelia's anger exploded! She had been struggling for hours to hang on to her self-control.

"If you don't control the magic, it will lead to your destruction," Luba spat.

Cornelia narrowed her eyes. "I don't remember asking for your advice!" she replied.

"You cannot dominate pure power," Luba hissed, "just as you cannot control the monstrous creature whom you would like to bring back to life!" She lifted her staff, its end glowing red hot, and pointed it at Caleb.

"Don't you go near him!" Cornelia shrieked. "I will not let you hurt him!"

"Stay back!" howled Luba. She lunged at Cornelia with the staff, and Cornelia tried to summon her own powers in return. But that proved to be too difficult. Cornelia crashed into the sliding doors behind her. The glass shattered, on the floor, and Cornelia was pinned to the door frame.

"How dare you challenge the symbol of Candracar's authority?" Luba roared.

"How dare *you*!" Cornelia bellowed.

Where was the Council of Elders in Candracar when I needed it? she wondered bitterly. She'd been obsessing over that question since the Veil had been repaired. "You all used me and my friends to defeat Prince Phobos," she rasped. "Caleb wasn't one of his servants! He was his enemy! So where were you when Phobos struck him down?"

Luba ignored her completely. "Surrender to the supreme authority, child! Don't make things worse for yourself!"

The end of her staff was alive with sparks.

Fwizz!

A sizzling sound echoed through the empty apartment. Cornelia was trapped.

Luba seemed to think she had the upper hand. "Give up your powers," she demanded, "before you lose control."

But it was way too late for that. Cornelia was blinded by the strength of her fury. She was stunned by her slip into pure emotion. Yet somehow she had finally got a grip on her power.

As Luba prepared to pierce Caleb with her staff, Cornelia's magic sizzled into her finger-tips. The power continued to grow. It engulfed her in a massive flare of white light, then created an impenetrable barrier around Caleb, just before the staff struck him.

"Leave me alone!" Cornelia croaked. She let out a scream that was rooted in her love and loss, her anger and hurt. Beams of light and magic careened around the room and coa-lesced in front of Luba.

Cornelia levitated toward the ceiling, shrouded in brilliant magic and beyond reach.

Then the floor of the apartment rippled, and from beneath its surface emerged a thick green vine, as sinuous as a rope. It resembled a snake preparing to strike. At Cornelia's command, the vine began to climb Luba's legs, wrapping itself tightly around them.

"Look at what you've become!" Luba taunted.

Cornelia was beyond all reason and beyond all shame.

Tu-tump!

Luba's staff clattered on the floor as the vine tied her hands.

Napoleon cowered under an armchair.

"Aaarrgh!" was all Luba could manage to squawk before she was completely bound by Cornelia's vine, silenced by the fearsome magic.

Cornelia continued to rise above Luba in a burst of brilliant light. Her magic was intense, pure, and powerful.

She just had no idea just how powerful she had become. . . .

THREE

What is going on? Luba thought as she struggled in her vine prison. *That blonde Guardian has rendered me powerless, imprisoning me in a vine as thick and as strong as a tree trunk. Now I lie on the floor of a wretched apartment in Heatherfield, a loathsome cat grinning at my disgrace. It is almost too much to bear.*

The Guardian had slipped away, holding the flower in her hands. She spoke to it lovingly, calling the flower Caleb.

But he is nothing more than a Murmurer, Luba thought. *A Murmurer. This Caleb was once an ally of Prince Phobos. He must never be trusted again!*

Luba tried to move her arms, then winced. It was hopeless. She lay in a stiff cocoon, only her neck and head free of the vine's itchy leaves and tight embrace.

My mind is working, even if my limbs are not, Luba thought. There's that to be grateful for.

Now there would be plenty of time to contemplate the chain of events that had led her to this humiliating position in the Guardian's lair.

It had all started when Luba was observing the Aurameres in the Temple of Candracar. It was a mind-numbing task to begin with, Luba recalled, but it was her duty. Day in and day out, she stood at her post in the Aura Hall, watching the Aurameres revolve around the room. The Aurameres were five shining spheres of magical essence, each representing a power held by one of the Guardians.

Luba had always harbored grave concerns about the newly appointed Guardians, so she did not love tending the Aurameres. Still, she did her chore faithfully, and, when the Aurameres changed, Luba took note. Gradually, the spheres had begun losing their size and brilliance. That, she realised, could mean only one thing: that the Guardians' powers were fading away. It was just as Luba had always expected. But she did not gloat – no . . . she simply brought the problem to the Oracle's attention.

And had the Oracle heeded her warning? As she thought about what had happened next, Luba's pulse quickened. Foolishly, the Oracle had not! For some reason, he was utterly enamored with the five teenagers he had chosen. No matter that they were silly, irresponsible, and immature girls, Luba fumed. No matter that they were not up to the job. Luba had tried to explain this to the Oracle in a hundred different ways. He had heard her, but he had not listened! Instead, the Oracle had stalled.

And soon Luba had come to a terrible realisation: she had to take matters into her own hands.

Through a reflecting pool in the Aura Hall, Luba could see the Guardians in Heatherfield and predict when they were about to unite their powers. One day, she spotted them in an office building, trying to work magic on a safe so that they could get at what was inside. As usual, Luba huffed to herself, the Guardians were using their powers for their personal gain.

As Luba stood guard in the Aura Hall, four

of the five Aurameres flew toward one another, as they always did when the powers were joined with that of the Heart of Candracar. One Auramere – the one corresponding to the blonde Guardian who was now her captor – continued to spin alone. But Luba could not wait for all five of the spheres to come together. If she was to save the world from the Guardians' folly, she couldn't lose any time!

Alone in the Aura Hall, Luba wove the four Aurameres together with her magic. And when the Heart of Candracar was summoned, the spheres fused together in a magnificent explosion.

Luba intended to blame the damage on the young Guardians. It was certainly possible that the powers of the dim-witted children could have self-destructed like that. Then she discovered that her intervention had had an unintended consequence: the melded powers had taken on a life of their own! The powerful spheres had assumed the form of an Altermere, a shape-shifting mass of pure energy, dead set on finding the fifth power again, to make itself complete.

Luba hated to admit it, but she'd made a big

mistake. When the five powers came together, one Guardian would wind up with unimaginable strength.

It was only a matter of time before the Altermere succeeded in finding Cornelia. After all, the Altermere would search everywhere for the fifth power, so that it could become complete. There was an undeniable force motivating the Altermere. It embraced the Guardian there in the doorway of that very apartment, Luba realised, transferring the power of all of the Guardians to her alone.

Now Cornelia carries the power of all four elements – plus the Heart itself.

In Candracar, criticism had rained down on Luba for what she had done.

They embarrassed me, she thought. They put me on trial. But I have no regrets. I opened their eyes! The weakness of the Guardians is now apparent for all to see: the way they misuse their powers; the way they fail to see dangers that are right in front of them. The fate of the world rests in their incapable hands? Not for much longer, if I can help it.

Luba couldn't even wiggle her pinkie at that moment. But she dared to hope she would escape. And she took great solace in what had happened at her trial.

Luba had not known what to expect when she strode into the Council's circular chamber to await its verdict. The Oracle had begun to speak in his most soothing voice. "The Council has not forgotten your invaluable services, Luba," he intoned. Luba had stood with her arms folded, barely concealing her disgust.

She'd been so focused on the way she was being treated that she had almost missed the Oracle's next words.

"You will therefore have the chance to atone for what you've done," he had declared. "You will go to Heatherfield. You will resolve the catastrophe that you have caused!"

I did all the right things, Luba told herself. I acted grateful and contrite, staring at the floor for an appropriate interval before shuffling out of the chamber. But I was joyful inside, not sorry in the least. They understood! They gave me a second chance! To fix my mistake . . . but I will never atone.

Luba had flinched when the Oracle put his hand upon her shoulder. "And I beg of you, dear friend. . . . Do not betray the trust that has been placed in you," he had said.

Luba recalled that Yan Lin had been at his side during the conversation. Yan Lin was a trusted friend of the Oracle's, but she was also the grandmother of Hay Lin, Guardian of the air.

Did he suppose I didn't know her bias? Luba wondered. *I could not resist taunting the Oracle a bit, not with Yan Lin standing right there.* Luba grinned as she thought of her performance.

"I won't disappoint you!" she had said subserviently. Then she'd assumed a sweeter tone. "But what will become of the other Guardians, Oracle?" They had lost their powers. Surely, Luba thought, the Oracle would have to act.

But he'd only snapped, "The Council has spoken, Luba!" Luba's sentencing was over – and so was the conversation.

Luba turned those memories over in her mind, trying to make sense of them. She came to the same conclusion every time.

I was given another chance, she told herself. *A part of the Council is behind me. A part of the Council agrees that we must no longer be hoodwinked by these girls! And if the Oracle* won't do anything, then I will.

The vines were cutting into Luba's wrists. She was beginning to feel pain – but she felt positively giddy with delight.

The Guardians will be replaced, and soon, she thought. The Council must realise it. I have a feeling that the Oracle is about to realise his mistake as well. The moment of change is finally at hand!

FOUR

As Irma walked home from Cornelia's apartment, she kicked a stone along the pavement. She couldn't care less where she was headed, as long as it was away from Cornelia, Hay Lin, and Taranee.

What do they think I am? fumed Irma. A lemming?

She was pretty sure that that was what those creatures who lined up and jumped off cliffs were called. Each one thoughtlessly did whatever the lemming in front of it did – even if it didn't seem like such a smart move.

Well, I'm no lemming, Irma seethed. I have a mind of my own, thank you very much. And I'm going to use it. I don't have to take it when someone slams a door in my face.

Friends shouldn't act that way – and neither should Guardians.

Irma crossed a street, then stopped to zip up her orange jacket. Summer vacation was about to begin, but summer hadn't started yet. The sun was going down, and it was definitely getting a little chilly.

She quickened her pace. Her mind was going almost as fast as her feet.

I was the only one of us to actually see the energy blob up close and personal, Irma thought. And I didn't go and get all wacky like Cornelia. Couldn't the girl show a little backbone? What was with passing out on the floor like that? And for that matter, couldn't she get a sense of humour? I've joked about her other-worldly boyfriends before, but now, suddenly, Cornelia has turned into Miss Supersensitivity. It's really too bad she can't take a joke.

Irma turned a corner and stomped down another block. I'm not going to let that ice queen treat me like dirt, she vowed. Then she giggled to herself.

Technically, I'm the ice queen, because I'm the one with water power. And Cornelia's dirt, because she's the earth girl.

Irma felt a little better knowing that.

It's not only that I'm not mad, she said to herself. Maybe it's because we're spending way too much time together. Maybe I need to start hanging out with different people . . . add a little variety to my life . . . spice things up.

Slowing her pace, Irma realised she wasn't anywhere near the park, where she had planned to be. She looked up and saw that she had ended up in front of the steps of the Heatherfield Museum.

The site of the world's worst date, Irma remembered. Way back when her magic was in full force, she'd skipped out of town to take care of some business in Metamoor. She'd left an astral drop, or magical double, in Heatherfield.

And, boy, did that astral drop get me into trouble, Irma chuckled. I *still* can't believe that my astral drop had the nerve to accept a date with Martin Tubbs, the geekiest boy in school! Talk about major backfire!

Irma couldn't get out of the date – not with her mum on her case. So she'd actually gone to the museum with Martin. And he'd turned out not so bad – once Irma had set him straight about her just-friends policy. Now Martin even tutored Irma in French. But he still had an annoying crush on her, and in no way was he boyfriend material.

The Heatherfield Museum sat on the edge of a cove. Its tall white pillars gleamed in what was left of the sunset, their reflections shining in the clear water. Sometimes, when she felt like a brief water break, Irma hiked around the stony bluffs behind the museum. But tonight was the perfect night for walking on the beach. Either way, being near a body of water always put Irma in a better frame of mind. And right now, she really felt like cooling down.

Irma walked past the museum, clambering over some large rocks. At the top of one particularly large boulder, Irma paused to take in her surroundings.

On the other side of the building, a broad expanse of sand opened up. She stood on the edge of the beach, gazing out at the view.

The soothing rhythm of the waves is the best sound in the world, Irma thought, watching the moon rise in the distance. This is where I *really* belong. This is who I *really* am. If only I knew who my real friends were, too.

Irma shook off those thoughts and headed out along the beach. She noticed a bunch of figures huddling around a bonfire nearby, but didn't think much of it till she drew closer and saw that it was a group of kids her age . . . and by then it was too late.

"Oh, sweet vision! My heart soars!" said a boy's voice, cracking painfully.

The one and only Martin Tubbs was running up to her.

As Martin sprinted toward her, sand flew behind him. "Hey, cupcake!" he shouted enthusiastically.

Irma took a long, hard look at him. It was nighttime. It was the end of the school year, and yet Martin was still wearing his Explorer Scout uniform. And it was the whole getup: shorts to the knees, buttoned flaps on the shoulders, a kerchief around the neck. Dork city.

Martin is always so eager to please – maybe he'll let me get away, Irma thought hopefully. She bent her head, stared at the sand, and stuck her hands in her pockets. "Martin . . ." she pleaded.

She should have known better than to hope

she might have been able to slip away. Clearly, this was a big moment for Martin.

"This is incredible!" he gushed. "How come your pals aren't with you?"

My pals? Irma thought. Guess he means Will, Taranee, Cornelia, and Hay Lin. Irma stumbled over the question for obvious reasons.

Can I really tell Martin we argued in the aftermath of an attack by a blue blob? she thought. Irma stuck with the short version. "Well . . . it's because . . . we had a fight."

Martin clapped a hand over his mouth. "Oops! I'm sorry! I shouldn't have asked!"

Serves you right for being nosy, Irma thought. Then she added silently, And now I'm getting mad all over again. But for some reason, even though she was annoyed, Irma couldn't resist telling Martin more. *Anybody* could see that she had been right to storm off. "We haven't been seeing eye to eye for a while now, so . . ."

Martin's hands flew wildly in the air as he gestured for her to stop. "Please, please, sweet thing!" he begged. "Please don't tell me any more! You don't have to explain! I don't care.

All I care about is . . . well . . . you know. . . ."

I definitely don't want to go *there*, Irma thought, cringing. "Well!" she said awkwardly, trying to avoid Martin's words. "Thanks, Martin! Ok, then . . ."

I'll just put one foot in front of the other now, she thought.

"Come on, Martin! Get over here!" a voice called from the bonfire.

Saved! Irma cheered inwardly as she hurried away. Glancing back, she saw that the voice belonged to a blonde girl. In the flickering light, Irma could see that the girl was wearing an outfit just like Martin's. Have I interrupted some kind of meeting? Irma wondered.

She began to walk away again. But she didn't get too far before a boy's voice chastised the girl. "Don't bother Tubbs!" the boy called. "Can't you see he's scoring points?"

Irma's temper flared all over again. That's it! she thought. Nobody's scoring points here – except me! She wasn't in the mood to be teased. Irma wheeled around and pointed at the boy who'd just spoken.

"You mean to tell me that someone like you would be an expert in scoring points?"

Martin's friends were the ultimate Outfielders at school – the polar opposite of the Infielders, or cool kids. Irma hadn't even seen these kids before. She doubted they were red hot on the dating scene.

The blonde girl laughed. "Direct hit! Chalk one up for . . ."

She doesn't know who I am, either, Irma guessed.

Martin was only too happy to fill her in. "For Irma!" he exclaimed. "She's a friend of mine!"

With the emphasis on *friend*, Irma added silently.

Suddenly the girl was next to Irma, patting her on the back. "Well, that means she's our friend, too! Anyone who can manage to make Doyle shut up is our pal!"

Guess Doyle's the guy who mentioned scoring points, Irma thought.

Martin popped out from behind the blonde girl and got right up in Irma's face.

If only he wasn't such a close talker, she thought. . . .

Flecks of saliva flew out of his mouth as he made his generous offer. "Come on!" Martin exclaimed. He grinned widely. "Why don't you join the Happy Bears?"

Ah, Irma realised. That explained the clothes. The Happy Bears were some kind of scout group Martin was in. She wasn't sure what they did, but obviously they had meetings and uniforms. Irma wouldn't have been surprised if the group had had a secret handshake or special code.

The blonde girl's eyes opened wide. "Do you want to become a Baby Bear?" she asked Irma breathlessly.

"Um . . . sounds like I might be a bit too old. . . ." Irma replied.

But, of course, it wasn't that easy. Martin spelled it out for her: "Baby Bears are new members of the Happy Bears! We'd be honored if you joined."

"Ummm," Irma said as she stalled for time.

In your dreams, she thought at first. But I *was* just thinking about branching out, she remembered. Without W.I.T.C.H. tying me down, well, the sky's the limit. I can do anything I want. Hey, I'm always up for an adventure. Nothing to lose by trying.

Irma shrugged. "Why not? Count me in!"

Martin's eyes bugged out. "Really?" It seemed as though she'd made his day. His week. His year.

The blonde girl snapped into action, pushing Irma toward the bonfire. "Ok, who's got an extra badge? As of tonight, the Happy Bears have a new member!"

Irma saw some other Bears slouching around the fire.

A minute ago I would have called it a convention of losers, Irma thought. But now I'm keeping an open mind.

A tall, skinny guy spoke up from the other side of the fire. Carefully, he examined the multitude of badges on his chest. "I've got one," he said, "But it's really old!"

"If it's rusty, all the better," Irma said. She couldn't keep from smirking. "It'll give me a look of seniority!"

Irma wondered how the boy could find the right badge in the dim light of the fire. But maybe he knew them by heart or something. In a flash, it was off his uniform and pinned to Irma's jacket. The tarnished, dirty badge looked odd against Irma's shiny orange jacket. A definite clash of styles, she decided. Like me and

Martin's crowd. But it was too late to back out now.

"Welcome to our group," the Happy Bears said in unison. Then they sat down and stared intently at the roaring fire.

Now what? Irma wondered. Is this what they always do? This is so not me.

Finally, after what felt like forever, somebody spoke up. "To celebrate, how about we play a round of Summerbummer?"

Martin looked at her expectantly "Want to play?" he asked.

Irma drew a blank. "What is it, exactly? The name makes it sound kind of weird. . . ." Her voice trailed off.

"It's a game about the summer-school courses we'll have to take!" the blonde girl explained.

Say no more! thought Irma. Nobody knew more about summer school than she did. "Then I'm sure to win!" she bragged. "Don't hurt yourself with your wild applause, but I'm going to end up with three classes! I can just imagine Mrs. Knickerbocker's face!"

Irma jumped up and did her best impression of Mrs. Knickerbocker, the principal of

Sheffield Institute (and the reason that it always felt right to call the place the Sheffield Institution). Irma stuck her rear end up in the air, suggesting Mrs. Knickerbocker's massive hindquarters. She wagged her finger and made her voice sound old and creaky. "Miss Lair, we expected more from you!"

The Happy Bears cracked up, and suddenly Irma felt a warm sort of glow. She'd been fighting with her other friends a lot lately. It had been a while since anyone had appreciated her excellent sense of humour.

When the laughter died down, however, Martin got all serious on her. It looked as though it killed him to contradict her, but Martin was all about rules. "The winner isn't the one who has to take the most courses," he said patiently. "The winner is the one who can guess how many the others will have to take!"

Scratch the warm fuzzies, Irma thought.

"I see," she said, stroking her chin, pretending to take it all in. "Now it's clear how you win. But can I ask you *what* you win?"

The rest of the Happy Bears looked at her. Apparently winning this game wasn't really the point. Irma sank down in the sand and stared into the glowing fire. Then she looked over at Martin, who was grinning at her. Even though Martin was annoying at times, right now it was nice to be around people who would laugh at her jokes and smile at her.

Irma wrapped her arms around her legs and huddled closer to the fire as she waited for the game to begin. Right now she wanted to be a Happy Bear.

FIVE

Will's feet were up on the dining-room table. Her favourite Karmilla tune was blasting in the background. For once, her mum wasn't objecting to either of those infractions of house rules. And, to top it all off, there was one slice of pizza left from their impromptu party, and it had Will's name written all over it.

Ahhh, sighed Will. If only things around here were always so peaceful. If only we always had so much to celebrate!

So how am I going to tell my friends my good news? Will wondered. I could call everyone and tell them that I'm not leaving Heatherfield . . . but who should I call first? And how will I ever get through to Cornelia?

Will grinned. Who'd have guessed, she

thought, that, this morning, these would be my biggest problems?

Just a few hours ago, we were walking into the Simultech building, Will remembered. Hay Lin, Taranee, Irma, and me. We were mistakenly blowing up my mum's boss's office and creating some blue energy creature. Boy, we really botched that mission.

Mum was pretty steamed about what happened, Will mused, and she doesn't even know the half of it! She was just mad that we were nowhere to be found when the fire alarm went off – and I sure wasn't about to tell her it was all our fault.

Will thought back to their car ride home. Her mum had launched into a superserious talk, and Will was sure she was doomed. But she wasn't grounded. Her allowance wasn't suspended. No . . . her mum had something much bigger on her mind. She'd decided they weren't leaving Heatherfield after all!

Will was still wrapping her mind around the news. Another major upheaval in her life? Not going to happen. The Vandoms were here to stay!

Too bad my mum didn't tell me a little

sooner, Will thought drily. If I hadn't tried to get my hands on that letter of resignation that my mum wrote to her boss, I could have saved Simultech a big cleanup bill. But it doesn't matter now. The important thing is that we're staying!

Now I'll turn over a new leaf, Will promised herself. I'll get straight A's in school. I'll go swimming every day. I'll take out the trash and clean my room.

Or maybe I should be a little more ambitious, she realised. Now I can get to know Matt Olsen a lot better. I'll work more hours at the pet store and hopefully have more time to hang out with him. Matt seemed to like dropping in on his grandfather's pet shop for visits. Maybe someday he'll be more than just a crush.

More importantly, though, Will knew that she had another mission.

I need to figure out what happened to our power – if I can't do it, Will thought, nobody can. As the leader of W.I.T.C.H., I am the one who should know what is going on with the Heart of Candracar and the other Guardians. I need to find a way to reach out to Cornelia. And I'll make sure we complete our next mission, whatever it is. If there is one. . . .

Will's mum poked her head out from the kitchen, interrupting Will's train of thought. She had another surprise up her sleeve: dessert! Will couldn't remember the last time her mum had whipped up a batch of chocolate-chip cookies, but there they were, piping hot. Will bit into one greedily, savouring the melted chips. Mmmm, she thought, standing in the middle of the living room and gazing out the window at the starry sky. Could any moment be sweeter than this one?

"I was thinking, Mum," she said with her mouth full. "From now on, everything's going to be perfect!"

"Of course!" her mum said brightly. "If we trust each other a little more!"

I really mean it! Will wanted to shout. She felt terrible about the way she'd been fighting with her mum. It wasn't easy for her mum to move to Heatherfield in the first place, Will knew.

And then, she thought, I had to go and get a top secret job saving the universe.

Will wished that she could share this secret with her mum, but she knew that she couldn't.

Now Will's mum walked across the plush red living-room rug, extending a hand to Will. "What do you say?"

After all they'd been through, all was forgiven. Her mum was giving her another chance. A fresh start. A clean slate.

Will was speechless. It was exactly what she wanted, but she couldn't think of anything to say. Her mum looked all excited, as though she were giving Will a precious gift. And she was.

I will make her proud, Will thought. A handshake won't be enough to seal the deal.

So, Will flew across the room and threw her arms around her mother. "I love you, Mum!" she gushed.

But Will was a little too gung ho. The force of her movement knocked her mum backward onto the sofa.

"Hey . . . hey!" her mum cried. "I'd forgotten what your outbursts of joy were like!"

Will squeezed her in a supertight hug, and her mum laughed. "Will," she said. "This is going a bit too far!"

Just then, there was a loud crash behind them. In her flying leap, Will had caused a lamp to topple and fall off the coffee table. Now it lay in fragments on the floor.

Great, Will thought. Just like me. Mum reaches out – and I knock her down and break something.

"I'll get the broom!" she volunteered quickly. "I am so, so sorry!"

Moments later, as they gingerly picked up the pieces, Will's mum shook her head. "You're unbelievable," she joked. "How do you manage to cause trouble just by hugging me?"

"I don't know," she said, a little embarrassed. "But I'll make you a promise!" She put her right hand over her heart and recited: "From now on, my room will always be perfectly clean. It'll shine! It'll sparkle! You'll be able to eat off the floor!"

Will's mum grinned. "A likely story," she replied.

"I'll even cook! And I'll sew my own buttons back on!" Will added, sweeping the last pieces of the vase off the floor.

"You mean you can actually tell a needle and thread apart?" her mum quipped.

If only I could bottle the feeling I have right now, Will wished. It's just like old times. Maybe new times will be like old times, too. Lighthearted. Relaxed.

She sighed contentedly.

Riiiing!

The shrill of the doorbell ringing broke Will's train of thought.

"Were you expecting someone?" Mum asked.

"No, but, whoever it is, it will be a nice surprise!" Will said, dancing toward the sound. "Today, nothing can go wrong!"

Will unlocked the door and opened it. Hay Lin stood in the hall, looking very worried. She had dark circles under her eyes, and there was a deep frown on her face.

Did I speak too soon? Will wondered.

All the happiness and positive feelings drained from Will's body. Something was wrong. Very wrong.

Hay Lin's voice was hushed. "We need you!" she said urgently. "It's important! You have to convince your mum to let you go out!"

Oh, no, Will thought, tonight of all nights! My mum will never let me out. But another look at Hay Lin was all she needed to reconsider. Hay Lin was usually so upbeat and carefree. She was like the element she controlled, breezy and calming air. But now she was not looking so light and free. She looked more like a major storm front. It looked as though she had the weight of the world on her frail shoulders, and Will couldn't let her carry it alone.

What am I gonna do? Will wondered. Mum gets upset whenever I disappear with my friends. The timing just couldn't be worse.

She tried to buy some time. "I – I don't know if she'll let me! It's already late!"

Before Will could say anything more, her mum was next to her in the doorway.

"Will? Who is it?" she asked as she peered over Will's shoulder. "Oh, it's you! Hello, Hay Lin!" she said, recognising a familiar face.

Mum couldn't be friendlier, Will thought gratefully. But did Mum notice Hay Lin's panicked expression?

"Hi, Mrs. Vandom," Hay Lin stammered. "I'm . . . I just stopped by to ask Will if she . . . if she . . . if we could go . . . for a walk. . . ."

Will had to act fast. She couldn't let her mum see Hay Lin like that. Slamming the door, Will turned to her mum. She wanted to talk to her mum alone. Hay Lin would understand, she thought, rationalising her rude behaviour.

Brushing a strand of red hair out of her face for maximum eye contact, Will looked at her mum. "Can I, Mum?" she asked.

Her mum paused for a second, long enough to make Will feel guilty all over again.

But she must have seen how desperate Hay Lin looked, Will thought. She must know that I need to be with my friends.

"Will, just a moment ago we were talking about trust," her mum said in a serious tone. "It's a commitment we made to each other."

I'm sunk, Will thought, I can't please my mother, and I can't help Hay Lin. Will looked at her mother as she considered her request.

"So, if we want to get along like we always used to," her mother said slowly, "I want you back at ten, ok?"

Will gave her mum another bear hug – but she didn't knock her over this time. "Ok! Just enough time to grab some ice cream!" she promised.

Hay Lin took off running as soon as the door closed behind Will. She'd heard the conversation, Will figured when she caught up to her, because Hay Lin was smiling.

"Time for ice cream, huh?" she asked. "You'll have to get the biggest cone they've got, then! I'm afraid we've got a lot of work to do!"

Together they ran off down the street, and Will knew that the night had definitely switched from joyful to serious. And she was ready.

SIX

It's so quiet here it's eerie, Cornelia thought. Like I'm in a ghost town or something.

The air outside her apartment building seemed still, as if a storm were looming. And even the indoor air was suddenly still. Cornelia strained to hear a familiar sound, like the humming of the refrigerator or the beep of the washing machine, signaling that a load of wash was done. But there was nothing.

And nobody. When is everyone coming back? Cornelia wondered. Mum and Dad took Lilian to see a movie. But which one? And where?

Cornelia couldn't remember a single detail.

They're not the only ones who could wander in any second, Cornelia thought.

What about Hay Lin, Irma, and Taranee? I sent them away, but they could still be lurking in the hallway. Or the elevator. Or the lobby.

She was beginning to panic.

How did Luba get here? Cornelia thought. Was she followed? Will I be having any more unwelcome visitors from Candracar? What if they're caught on camera? Security is pretty tight around here. There are cameras everywhere. What would the guards make of cat-woman creeping into the Hales' apartment? What would they think of the broken window and the tattered curtains? *What would they think of the body on the floor?*

Cornelia forced herself to stare at the figure lying motionless on the rug.

Thick, dark vines were clenched so tightly around Luba that the tips of her fingers were slowly turning white. Her eyes were closed, and for a moment Cornelia was able to fool herself into believing that Luba was just sleeping.

Cornelia held her head in her hands. "What have I done?" she moaned. She could barely remember what had happened. She just knew that she'd felt an awesome surge of magic. That she'd been about to bring Caleb back to his human form. And that she'd blasted Luba, who got in her way.

It's like I turned into someone else, Cornelia thought, fretting. Like I lost my mind or something. Have I really harmed someone from Candracar? I am in deep trouble. And I am all alone.

Cornelia forced herself to approach Luba and speak. "I'm sorry I did this to you, Keeper of the Aurameres! I didn't mean to hurt you!"

I don't know what got into me, she added silently.

Cornelia noticed Napoleon blinking at her.

I know, she thought, looking at her cat, it's lame. But it's the best I can do right now, ok?

Cornelia cringed. At least I didn't answer the cat out loud, she thought. That would *really* be crazy.

What should I do? she wondered. I can't exactly call the police.

I guess I'll just have to sit back and wait. But I'm not sure for what.

And then she remembered: Caleb.

I felt him almost come back to me, she thought. I should try again.

Cornelia's cool and rational side reacted

immediately. What if there's more damage? This place is already a disaster zone.

But that cool and rational side was no longer in control.

I want him back – it's as simple as that, Cornelia decided. I need him. Now.

Sitting down on the floor, she took Caleb's vase in her hands. "I'm scared," she told Caleb honestly. "I'm totally confused."

She felt she had the power to change him. And suddenly she felt the energy begin to build up inside her again – it was as if somebody had flipped a switch and the magic had sprung back to life. Cornelia was overflowing with a passionate desire to see Caleb again. She was flooded with a new strength. And her determination was greater than ever. "I was so close before!" she said.

Cornelia jumped up, walked to a window, and stared out at the skyline of Heatherfield. "There's no turning back now," she said out loud. She was about to let the magic take control.

Returning to sit on the floor again, Cornelia tried to relax. She tried to keep an open mind. Now she knew there was no use in trying to guide her overwhelming power. This time, she would have to let it guide her.

Cornelia took a series of cleansing breaths and attempted to find a focus.

What can I think of while I let the magic grow? she wondered. And then, she knew. It was so obvious, it made her smile and her heart ache.

Cornelia travelled deep into her mind to dwell upon every moment she had ever spent with Caleb. She thought back to the dreams she'd had of him before they'd ever met; to the first time she had ever seen his kind eyes, his tousled hair, his beloved face. She relived every battle they'd fought together. She revisited every place they'd ever been. And she relived the very last moment they had held each other in Meridian.

Cornelia had stepped out of herself completely. Now the magic was in control. Her emotions were in control. All she knew was that she needed Caleb more than ever to help her through this mess. All she felt was the absolute certainty that, this time, her magic would come through.

I cannot fail, Cornelia thought.

Then, out loud, she said, very simply, "Now, Caleb, come back to me."

She stretched her hands toward the vase, as if by instinct.

Fzzzzz . . . fzzzzz . . . fzzzzz.

Caleb's stem sprang up an inch.

At first Cornelia felt only fear, mixed with a fair amount of doubt.

Did I imagine it? she wondered. *Could this really be working?*

But then the stem sprang up further. The flower that was Caleb was growing.

Cornelia was filled with an indescribable joy. Her power glowed as Caleb was slowly transformed. Her magic lit the room up like a sunrise.

Caleb's stem climbed high above the top of the vase without toppling it. The stem stretched toward the ceiling, and new branches sprouted. Soon it was far above Cornelia, who remained kneeling on the floor, clenching her hands in disbelief.

"It's happening," she breathed. "He is really coming back."

All at once Cornelia was distracted by something she saw from out of the corner of her eye. It was Napoleon, the cat, crouching near Luba's head, sniffing her face.

Anger exploded in Cornelia's mind like a flashbulb. That silly cat was always interfering and ruining her plans.

But then she saw that Napoleon was the least of her problems.

Luba was waking up!

Her eyes darted open, and Napoleon, startled, scampered away. The room returned to the strange, still silence.

Slowly Luba's hand began to twitch beneath the vines that bound her. She was struggling to break free. then, having freed one hand from the tangle of vines, she reached for her magic staff, which lay nearby. Luba looked intent as she held onto the staff. The powerful staff allowed her to free herself from the vines that had held her captive. With feline agility she leaped to her feet.

Cornelia froze, shocked.

Luba stomped toward Cornelia with her blue staff held tightly in her hand. She was bending at the waist, her cat lips parted to reveal a menacing smile. "It's over, child!" she shouted with glee.

"Oh!" Cornelia squeaked.

Paralysed, she watched as Luba leaped into the air, brandishing the staff high over her head. "In the name of the rulers of Candracar!" she screeched. "May the power of the earth return to silence!"

"N-o-o-o-o-o-o-o!" shrieked Cornelia. Luba tearing away her power was tearing away her heart.

"You've made your choice, Cornelia!" Luba roared. "From now on, you won't be able to make any more mistakes. . . ."

Mistakes? How could helping Caleb be a mistake?

". . . Because your power is no longer within you!" Luba continued. "It has abandoned you! Forever!"

Cornelia turned to look at Caleb. He was growing ever taller, ever stronger. His new branches were sprouting flowers. Instinct told her that Luba was lying.

But, as Cornelia grasped one of Caleb's blossoms with a trembling hand, the flower fell to the ground. Next, the new branches folded inward, and right before her very eyes Caleb began to shrivel away.

Cornelia could not think. She could only feel. From the core of her being, she felt rage course toward the surface. "What did you do to him?" she screamed in a voice she could not recognise.

"I warned you!" Luba yowled.

Those were the last words Cornelia heard before she was engulfed in a blaze of light and everything went silent.

SEVEN

And then there was one Guardian left, Taranee thought. Me.

Standing outside Cornelia's apartment building, Taranee looked at her watch. How long till Hay Lin returns with Will? she wondered. Where could they be? Taranee knew she would have to have completed the most important task by the time those girls arrived: getting Cornelia to open that door.

If we can get Cornelia to listen, there will be four of us, Taranee thought. Then we'll only have to locate Irma – and hope that she's cooled down by now.

As she approached the Hales' apartment building, Taranee felt a sudden longing for her power. She ached to start a fire again. The feeling of not being able to control fire was as painful as a broken bone and as persistent as a migraine.

I felt so brave when I had magic, Taranee thought, remembering. At first, the power freaked me out, but after a while it felt comfortable, like a part of me. I'm not me without my power. Or . . . I'm not the me I want to be. None of us are, she added grimly.

That was why Taranee was so determined to revive the Power of Five. She missed her magic power, but she missed her friends most of all – and the first step in getting them back was to get all of them together in one place.

And on speaking terms, preferably, Taranee thought with a smile. But, first things first. We can work on the whole speaking-thing later.

In the meantime, I have to stay upbeat, Taranee decided, since nobody else is. I need to keep looking on the bright side, to believe we can repair the damage and be a group again. I cannot lose sight of that goal.

Suddenly an old song popped into her head, one that her mum had used to sing when Taranee and her brother were little kids. Taranee didn't know all the words, but the catchiest part went, *Be positive, and buzz, buzz, like a baby bumble bee.* Taranee smiled to herself. It'll be my theme song!

Taranee strode through the large lobby, nodded to the doorman, and rode the elevator up to the penthouse floor.

The doorman didn't bother to announce her. He knew that Taranee was a friend of Cornelia's – she'd been there many times these last few days.

I just hope Cornelia still thinks of me as her friend and lets me in to talk to her, Taranee thought as she paused outside Cornelia's door. These days, no one knew what to expect from Cornelia.

Well, here goes nothing, Taranee said to herself. She took a deep breath and tried to calm her racing heart.

Taranee decided to begin with the most obvious thing: ringing the doorbell. She crossed her fingers and made a wish.

She heard the sound of the bell echo through Cornelia's cavernous apartment, but then there was silence. Taranee heard no footsteps coming to the door.

Well, she couldn't have missed that bell,

Taranee thought. She must be ignoring it.

Taranee tried knocking on the door, to no avail. Cornelia was not coming.

She knocked one more time, hoping that Cornelia was just being stubborn. Still, nothing.

Ok, Taranee said to herself. Time to try something different. I don't care if I embarrass myself, so long as I embarrass *her* into opening up the door.

Taranee knocked again, shouting. "Cornelia! Cornelia!"

Humming her theme song, the Bee Song, under her breath, Taranee tried the doorbell again. Although there was still no answer, she remained optimistic and persevered.

"Open up, Cornelia!" she cried.

Only silence greeted her.

"Why won't you answer?" Taranee yelled at the closed door.

Cornelia didn't bother to respond. But somebody else did.

A voice behind her wheezed, "Hey, you! Are you through making all that ruckus?"

Taranee whirled around to see a white-haired woman standing in the hallway frowning. "It's quite clear that Miss Hale is not at home," she said with a scowl.

Taranee stifled a giggle. *No wonder Cornelia's never introduced us to her neighbours,* she thought. Looking more closely at the woman, Taranee shook her head slightly. The neighbor was wearing a fur-lined purple coat over a delicate pink slip-dress that looked suspiciously like a nightgown. Several strands of pearls hung from her neck, and she wore a garish ring on every one of her fingers. The heels of her boots were so high they could hardly hold her up – Taranee could see her teetering. She wasn't sure if the lady had escaped from a horror flick or from high society, but she was definitely eccentric.

Taranee tried to explain herself: "Oh, no, I'm positive that Cornelia . . ."

The woman wouldn't let her finish. Before she had time to react, the woman grabbed Taranee's elbow with her brittle fingers. "This is a quiet building, young lady!" she hissed. "Shouldn't you be at home studying?"

"We don't have any homework for tomorrow," Taranee snapped, trying to sound braver than she felt.

The woman pointed her finger at Taranee.

Guess she's trying to look scary, Taranee thought. But she doesn't need to *try* – she already looks horrifying.

"That's no reason to spend the evening making noise in my building!" the woman growled. She stalked away, muttering "Little witch!" under her breath.

Taranee had to smile. You have no idea how much I wish that were true! she thought with a little chuckle.

Taranee was irritated by the interruption. Time was ticking away. She had to reach Cornelia. She returned her focus to the problem of the locked door. Cornelia was not opening up to talk to her. She had to come up with an alternate plan.

Feeling a familiar longing, she sensed that she was incomplete without her control over fire. She was determined to stay focused, though, and fought to stay like the baby bumblebee – positive.

Being a Guardian has changed me, and not just because of my ability to control fire, she thought. I am smart and strong. And right now I need to be creative. I can do this! The Oracle had faith in me – he chose me to be a Guardian and to control fire. He believes in me.

"Buzz, buzzzzz," Taranee hummed as she looked out a large window in the hallway and waited for the elevator to come.

What a gorgeous view, she thought. Not a bad place to escape from the world.

And there it was, just waiting for her.

The fire escape!

I could jump down to Cornelia's terrace, she realised. Why not try it out? With my powers, I'd have done it in an instant. No reason not to try that plan now.

The elevator doors opened, and Taranee rode back down to the lobby. Hoping not to attract attention, she left the building and walked around to the side that wasn't visible from the street. That was where the fire escape was, stretching all the way up to the top floor. Taranee started to climb the stairs quickly, trying not to look down, and trying not to lose her nerve.

When she finally reached the terrace of Cornelia's apartment, she was panting and out of breath. Then she noticed an open window. It was exactly the break she'd been needing!

Mum would call this unlawful entry, she

thought. And, actually, that's just what it is. But that won't stop me now.

Taranee scrambled in to the apartment and sneaked past the piano in the den.

I have a good reason to be here, she thought, arguing in her mind with her mother, whose grave face seemed to appear before her, looking disappointed.

Ok, I may not be able to convince her that I'm completely innocent in all of this, Taranee admitted to herself. Maybe I should start looking for a good lawyer!

Taranee felt lighthearted. She was about to find her friend, and she was pretty sure Cornelia wouldn't turn her away.

Suddenly, Taranee realised that somebody other than Cornelia was in the next room.

She heard a strange, gruff voice. Taranee couldn't quite place it, but it made the hair on the back of her neck stand up.

That doesn't sound like any of the Hales, Taranee thought. I haven't seen them in a while, but I think I'd recognise their voices.

At first, Taranee couldn't make out any words, but then, very clearly, she heard the voice bellow, "You should have listened to me!"

Cornelia is in trouble, Taranee thought. I have to check it out.

She crept to the doorway, slinked into the hall, and peered around the door to the living room, where she heard the voices.

Uh-oh, she thought, recoiling.

No wonder the voice had sounded strange. It was more alien, even, than that of the lady in the hall. It was an otherworldly voice. It was the voice of a being from Candracar!

Taranee couldn't remember where or when or why she knew the face. But she had seen the creature's whiskers before, and the features, somewhere halfway between a human's and a cat's.

What is *that* creature doing here in Heatherfield? Taranee thought, confused. It didn't make any sense.

The creature was screaming mysterious words at Cornelia: "Now it will be up to the Congregation to judge your foolish act!"

Cornelia stood in the centre of the room, her arms wrapped around a whirling mass of thick, colourful vines. Her eyes were shut, and her face held a determined, fierce look.

Taranee summoned up all the courage that

she possessed. "Cornelia!" she cried. "I'm here!"

But she was much too late.

Just then, the creature from Candracar, using the staff in her hand, produced a hot, bright light. The light catapulted across the room and swirled around Cornelia, enveloping her completely.

Then, in a flash, both the creature and Cornelia disappeared.

EIGHT

Inside the Temple of Candracar, Luba rubbed her hands together in anticipation.

Now the Guardian will realise how she has misused her powers, she chortled softly to herself. Now all will see her terrible mistake. Yes, the Guardian is exactly where I want her.

Cornelia was isolated in a distant corner of the Temple, where none from the Council of Elders would stumble across her.

I stripped her of her powers, Luba smirked to herself. But of course, I had to bring her here. It is much better to confront the foolish Guardian on my territory. I was ill at ease in her apartment, and certainly that location did not afford us much privacy!

Luba shook her head, remembering

the close call she'd had with Taranee.

No, it was best for the Guardian and me to be sure of having some time alone, she thought.

What is the Guardian doing now? Luba wondered. She turned to her reflecting pool and looked in, to observe what was happening in a chamber not very far away.

She saw the Guardian, hunched on the floor, sobbing piteously. The flower on which she had worked her magic was still at her side and still evolving.

Kshhh!

Fshhh!

Sounds filled the room as the form changed into its essential self.

Perhaps she thinks that without her powers, its metamorphosis will stop, Luba realised. But, of course, I have taken care of that.

A broad smile came over Luba's face. She had worked a little magic of her own. What happened next would be an unpleasant surprise for the girl. Restlessly, Luba waited for her scheme to come to fruition.

This moment has been too long in coming, she thought seethingly. At last I will have concrete evidence against the girl.

Then, at last, there was real movement. All at once, the green leaves of the flower fell away to reveal human features. It was a boy! A boy with green hair and green skin. The telltale complexion of a Murmurer, Luba thought, shuddering. Right there, in the centre of Candracar. Even the Oracle would not be able to forgive this!

Luba bent closer to the pool so as not to miss a moment of Cornelia's reaction.

The Guardian moved slowly as the flower shed its leaves. It was if she were walking through water or through a fog. It was as if she didn't believe her own eyes.

The Murmurer – known as Caleb to the girl – gurgled as his transformation ground to a stop.

The Guardian appeared to be in shock. Placing her hands on his chest, she stared into the Murmurer's glassy eyes. "No! It can't be!" she cried.

She expected Prince Charming, Luba gloated. Instead, she got a servant of the dark prince, Phobos – she got what her boyfriend always was, at heart.

The Guardian shook him. "Caleb, please!" she shouted. "Can you hear me?"

Then she took his face in her hands. She seemed ready to kiss him – but even then, she faltered. "Oh, no!" she whispered. "What have I done?"

Luba's spirits soared. It's every bit as glorious as I'd hoped! she gloated. When this Guardian had all the powers in the world, what has she chosen to do? Revive an enemy! What foolish behaviour! She *has* to be stopped!

Luba was so excited that she leaped to her feet. Surely, she thought, the Council will come down hard on her who has introduced the enemy into Candracar, stronghold of all that is right and good!

Luba smiled. And surely the Council would see that this Guardian was not the only one capable of such poor judgment! This girl had done what any of those Heatherfield girls would have done. They were all weak. If the Council knew what was righteous and correct, orders would be decreed to anoint new Guardians.

Luba was done waiting. It was time to confront the Guardian face to face and teach her what it meant to be a true and responsible Guardian.

She made her way to the chamber and unlocked the heavy door. "I hope you're satisfied!" Luba said to the girl.

Luba saw at once that the Guardian had not yet lost her arrogance. "You! Why don't you leave me alone?" Cornelia spat.

Luba reminded herself of what had to happen now: the girl would turn herself in to the Council, admitting her error. The Council would know only that the girl had used her magic for her personal affairs – and let it rage out of control. The Council would see only that she'd been tricked by a Murmurer.

"First, you have to understand the mistake you've made," Luba said, lecturing Cornelia.

Luba used her staff to prod the belly of the Murmurer. "Look at what your madness has created! You've brought back a monster!" Then she pointed the crook of the staff at Cornelia. "And you have become a monster, too!"

The Guardian scowled. "I made my decision and I was wrong," she finally conceded. "But this is your fault, too!"

Only she will ever guess that, Luba thought. And I shall never admit that I had a hand in this plot.

"Ha-ha-ha!" she hooted. "Grow up, child! Accept responsibility for your actions!"

The Guardian lashed out at her. "But you interfered with my power!" she cried. "I could have brought Caleb back to life!"

Yes, you could have, Luba thought. With your power over all the elements, you could have done whatever you chose. Luckily, you could not control such forceful magic. Luckily, you have no idea what you were capable of. Luckily, I stepped in at the critical moment!

Luba rolled her eyes and lowered her voice. She needed to get through to the girl. "So, you still don't understand?" she sighed. "The creature you speak of never existed!"

Luba watched as the Guardian's eyes filled with tears and her human lip trembled.

I've got her, Luba thought with pride. "He was just an illusion!" she went on. "One of Phobos's servants with a human appearance!"

Cornelia stammered, "You're . . . you're lying! That's not true! That can't be true!"

Luba waited to speak until an adequate interval had passed. She wanted the full horror of the Guardian's blunder to dawn on the girl. Cornelia had been granted the power to help protect Candracar and all that was good in the universe. Instead, she had brought evil into the very heart of the Temple of Candracar!

Finally, Luba broke the silence. "Caleb will end up in the dungeons of the Temple with the other Murmurers," she announced. "And now, you must decide which side you're on. Think it over, Cornelia! And remember that, by admitting your guilt, you will avoid being punished by the Council of Elders!"

Selfish Guardian, Luba silently added under her breath. Naturally, you will choose to protect your own hide and, perhaps, your powers. Unfortunately for you, though only I know that your powers are gone for good!

The Guardian turned her back on Luba, willfully ignoring her.

I have said my piece, thought Luba. I will be surprised if she does not see the wisdom of the course I propose. And now, I have other tasks to attend to!

Luba turned, leaving Cornelia to weep over the inert form of the Murmurer. She hurried back to the Aura Hall to take care of some important business. There was no time to waste.

When she arrived at the other side of the

Temple, Luba saw the Oracle sweep through an arched corridor with Yan Lin. While taking care to avoid being spotted by them, Luba overheard their conversation, which echoed in the stone passageway.

Yan Lin sounded perturbed. "I think that it's time for us to do something!" she said.

About Cornelia? Luba wondered nervously. How much do they know?

The Oracle sounded tired. "And on whose side, Yan Lin?"

Luba knew what the answer would be. She knew that Yan Lin would choose to intervene on the side of the Guardian. Yan Lin herself had been a Guardian, long ago. Now her granddaughter, Hay Lin, was a Guardian as well. How dare the Oracle ask for her guidance? Luba thought angrily.

"Do you feel that your opinion and that of the Council would coincide?" the Oracle asked Yan Lin.

So now he's polling the Congregation? Luba wondered. He is even weaker than I thought.

"I'll try to hold myself back. . . ." Yan Lin sighed.

She will not try to affect his decision now, at

least, Luba thought. She's still in awe of him, the fool! Well, Luba raged, Yan Lin can hold herself back for as long as she likes. I, however, will hold myself back no longer! For the good of Candracar, I cannot stand by and allow these Guardians to do any more damage! The Council is bound to rule first against Cornelia, then against the others. In the meantime, I shall take the next step.

Luba made her way to the Aura Hall, where once she had tended the Guardians' five Aurameres. Each Auramere mirrored the power of one of the Guardians; there was one for each of the girls. The enlarged, single Auramere that was now in the hall had been created when Cornelia absorbed the powers of the Altermere, the creature that held the powers of all her friends.

The disaster of the Altermere's creation was now over, and Luba had to finish the task at hand. Cornelia had absorbed the pure power of the Altermere that was made up of the four Aurameres when the creature had embraced Cornelia at her apartment. When that happened, her power was joined together with the Altermere's, giving rise to an outstanding magic that Cornelia had no idea how to manage. Later, when Luba awoke on Cornelia's floor, she drained the power from Cornelia with her magic staff.

Back in the Aura Hall, Luba knew what she had to do. She had to transfer all of the powers from her staff to the single Auramere that was left. Luba faced the sphere squarely and carefully positioned her staff.

She skillfully aimed the staff at the large sphere. Her magic whirled around the Auramere, creating an angry breeze which, in turn, covered – and then choked – the mass of energy. The all-powerful, supercharged, single Auramere exploded with an eerie scream, releasing a tornado of energy in all the colours of the rainbow.

When the air cleared, Luba could see five separate orbs, each of a different colour, circling around the room. The Auramere was again divided back into the five original orbs, just as it should be. It was as if the combined forces of the Aurameres making up the Altermere had never existed.

At that moment, Luba made a solemn proclamation to the empty Hall: "Now the time has come for the dispersed powers to shine once again within the Aurameres. . . ." she intoned, ". . . until five new Guardians are chosen!"

NINE

Irma propped herself up against a rock as the rest of the Happy Bears roasted marshmallows over the bonfire. The Bears were talking, laughing, and including her. Irma watched the four friends as they kidded each other and had a good time.

Hmmm. I used to be like that with Will, Hay Lin, Taranee, and Cornelia, Irma thought. I wonder what they – my old friends – are doing right now? Will's probably still fighting with her mum; what else is new? I bet Taranee and Hay Lin are still stuck in the Hales' lobby, squabbling over what to do. And Cornelia? She's probably showering her flower with kisses. Puh-leeze!

Irma glanced out at the water and at the

moonlight sparkling on the waves.

All right, she admitted to herself, the water-power thing was awesome. But I don't have to be friends with those girls 24-7. No way will I put myself in a box! Not when there's a whole world out there. Not when I have so much to offer. I'm still glad I've decided to explore new horizons.

She looked over at the Happy Bears and took a deep breath.

Nope, wouldn't trade this for all the world, she thought. I mean, it's not a rip-roaring good time or anything. But Martin's crowd is ok. No high-stakes battles. No personality clashes. Who needs best friends? Watching the waves here with the Bears. . . . It's relaxing.

She turned to regard Martin sitting cross-legged in the sand, his skinny legs glistening in the light of the fire. He looked up at Irma with adoring eyes.

"So, Irma, having fun?" he asked.

In a way, she thought. But she didn't want to let him get too excited.

Next thing you know, she thought, he'll have me running for Bear Chief!

"I'll tell you. . . ." Irma began. "You Happy

Bears are really nice!" She shrugged. It was an honest and true statement.

The blonde girl next to Martin objected to Irma's answer. "Nice? That's it?" she complained. "I thought you found us completely cool!"

Irma smiled. Not cool, for sure. But not awful, either.

Before she could reply, another Happy Bear piped up. He had squinty eyes and a strange hairdo that Irma could only think of as a grave fashion faux pas. "She'll think we're just fantastic after a round of Egghead!" he bragged. "Did you all bring eggs?"

Eggheads playing Egghead, Irma thought. Figures.

The Happy Bears rushed to their backpacks and rooted around in them. Soon each had produced an egg, and soon all the eggs were placed in a box on top of a towel.

Irma stifled a fit of the giggles. Were they going to dye the eggs? Eat them raw? What kind of game was this?

She looked over at Martin. "Should I be worried?" she whispered.

"Are you kidding me?" Martin was

practically jumping up and down.

Obviously, Irma thought, throwing up her hands.

"It's one of our favourite games!" Martin exclaimed. "It's easy!" He put his arm around her shoulder, and Irma quickly wriggled away. "You just tie a blindfold around your head, and you choose an egg. Then you whack it against your forehead! If it's hard-boiled, you win, but if it isn't . . ."

Martin left the rest to her imagination.

Irma gulped. *Gross,* she thought. Then she remembered that she was supposed to be keeping an open mind. Could be a lot worse, she decided. At least the Bears don't want to go skinny-dipping.

It was too late to get out of the game, anyway, because the Bear next to her was grinning. "Can I offer you one of my handkerchiefs?" he asked.

I have got to be a good sport, Irma considered. She even let Martin tie it on. She pushed the blindfold up on her forehead so she could watch the scene.

A little farther down the beach, the game had begun. The blonde girl chose the largest egg she could find and smacked it on her forehead. The egg cracked! Bits of yellow yolk oozed down the girl's face, gluing pieces of eggshell to her skin. The girl seemed cheerful enough about it. "I lost!" she said as the other Bears cracked up.

Irma's stomach flip-flopped.

Whatever you do, you can't throw up, she said to herself. Being here is embarrassment enough. You cannot further embarrass yourself in front of the Bears.

It was Martin's turn next. He slammed the egg into his forehead, and the same thing happened: total breakage. "Oops!" he shouted.

The Bears started guffawing again. They were starting to get on Irma's nerves.

"It's your turn, Dexter!" called the Mohawk boy. Dexter was the most bearlike of the Happy Bears, Irma thought, large and round with reddish hair.

"You bet!" said Dexter. "One . . . two . . . three!"

Cronck! went the egg as it hit his forehead.

"Ugggh!" cried Dexter. His eyes seemed to roll back in his head. Then he fell face first into the sand!

What happened? Irma wondered. Is he ok?

Nobody else seemed too concerned. The other Happy Bears rolled around laughing as though what had just happened were the funniest thing they'd ever seen.

I don't think Dexter seems like the coolest guy, either, Irma thought. But that is downright mean!

"The stone egg! The stone egg!" yelled one of the Bears as she caught her breath.

Irma had to know. "Stone egg? Wh – what would that be?"

The Bear next to her had tears streaming down his face from laughing so hard. He wiped his eyes with the back of his hand. "You know," he said. "One of those egg-shaped granite ones. We always hide one in the pile!"

Yeah, and I always hide one in the egg carton in the fridge, Irma fumed. She was trying to branch out; she was trying to think positive. But she just couldn't let this go.

"This is all so stupid!" she exploded. "How can you guys find this fun?"

The Happy Bears fell silent and glared at her.

Even Martin looked upset by her outburst.

"But, honey-bunny, we're Happy Bears!" he said, as if that explained everything. Their dumb uniforms. Their silly games. Their warped sense of humour.

Doyle dared to sidle up to her with an egg. He had the nerve to borrow Martin's nickname. "Your egg, honey-bunny," he said. "If you want to be one of us, you know what you have to do!"

I sure do! Irma thought gleefully. She took the egg from his hand and broke it on his head! "It's raw, Doyle!" she yelled. "You lose!"

Irma had had it with that crowd.

Will I ever find a place where I fit in? she wondered. Then she shook the thought off. This is no time to get all existential, Irma decided. I have to get out of here!

Irma tore the handkerchief off her forehead and smoothed down her hair. As she walked back toward the museum, she turned and waved to Martin. "See you around!" she said.

Martin almost fell to his knees. "Sweetie-cakes!" he begged. "You're leaving us, just like that? But we're the Happy Bears! We're your good friends!"

Irma shook her head. She felt a little bad,

but there was no point in beating around the bush. "Thanks, Martin!" she said. "But I already *have* four good friends!"

Martin didn't answer, and Irma didn't see his reaction, because she was running down the beach toward the museum.

Four good friends, she repeated to herself. If only I can find them!

TEN

Hay Lin's sneakers squeaked on the pavement as she ran through Will's neighborhood. She raced past fire hydrants and lampposts and finally down a dark alley, the fastest way she knew to Cornelia's place.

Glancing over her shoulder, Hay Lin made sure Will was still in sight. Will's a much better swimmer than she is a runner, Hay Lin thought, watching her friend's uneven strides. I'm much lighter on my feet! she thought.

But Will was still behind her. There was no time to talk to Will and fill her in on the huge fight Irma and Cornelia had had and how strange Cornelia had been acting. All that really mattered now was that Hay Lin get her to Cornelia's apartment.

I promised Taranee I'd deliver Will, Hay Lin remembered.

Hay Lin had no idea what Taranee was planning once the two of them arrived at the Hales'. But four of them would be together again. Hay Lin was almost bursting with excitement, she loved the idea so much. Sure, Cornelia could be difficult and all that, she mused. But they shouldn't have let her stay away so long. It just wasn't right. They needed to be a team!

If only we could fly to Cornelia's! she wished. Running takes so long!

And if I still had my powers, I would be able to do just that, Hay Lin thought. This whole no-powers thing really stinks.

After they had gone a few more blocks, they finally turned in to Cornelia's apartment complex. Hay Lin jogged into the lobby and waited for Will near the elevator. She didn't have to wait long. The elevator doors opened just as Will arrived, panting and red-faced, and together, the two rode silently up to Cornelia's floor.

Relief flooded over Hay Lin when they reached the Hales' front door. It looked as if

Taranee had found a way in after all. The door was open.

But Hay Lin's great mood crashed as soon as she walked into the apartment.

The place was a shambles.

The curtains were shredded. The window was broken. The floor was covered with pieces of broken glass. Nothing had been left undamaged. Even the glass covering the pictures on the wall had been shattered.

Taranee was there, chewing on her fingernails.

Cornelia was nowhere in sight.

This was not the scene that Hay Lin had expected to see.

Taranee's voice quavered as she explained what she'd seen and heard. The cat-woman from ˙Candracar, screaming at Cornelia. Something about being judged by the Council. Then the cat-woman and Cornelia vanishing in a blaze of light.

Hay Lin listened and felt her shoulders slump.

Just when things were looking up, she thought a little bitterly. I wonder what's in worse shape: Cornelia's apartment, or W.I.T.C.H.?

Taranee threw up her hands. "If we had our powers, we could straighten everything out!" she said.

Biting her lip nervously, Hay Lin pretended to examine a damaged curtain. She didn't know what the three of them could do at that point – if they could do anything at all.

But Will, the constant leader, wasn't about to let a little house-wrecking get in her way. With a detemined look in her eye, she glanced over at Taranee and Hay Lin. "If we had our powers, we'd start looking for Cornelia!" she said. "Let's get out of here!"

Will led the way back through the same lobby that Hay Lin had been in about a million times that day already.

At least someone has a plan, Hay Lin thought. But she doubted they could find Cornelia. Where do we even start? she wondered. Cornelia could be anywhere with the cat creature.

Hay Lin lagged behind as Taranee and Will walked down the path toward a gate leading out of the apartment complex. She couldn't stop thinking about what her friends had said.

If we had our powers, this; if we had our powers, that, she thought. What happened to our magic, anyway? Where did it go?

Thinking back over the last few days, Hay Lin tried to remember when everything had changed. When was the last time that they had used their powers successfully?

Then she remembered.

"Our powers have been completely gone since that blob appeared at Simultech!" she cried.

"Yeah!" Taranee agreed. "Sure looks that way."

"Something's changed," Will declared. "All I know is that when we were united, we were strong!"

Hay Lin nodded.

When we stuck together, we could still make the magic work, Hay Lin thought. We could still fight . . . and win.

"Then we started fighting," Taranee said, interrupting Hay Lin's thoughts. "And our powers faded away little by little until they vanished completely."

"At Simultech, we *were* together," Hay Lin said. "And look what happened there."

"Cornelia was missing," Will said quietly, pointing out what they didn't want to acknowledge.

She's right, Hay Lin thought. But what is she saying? Our magic worked even without Cornelia. How can that be?

It took Hay Lin a moment to put two and two together. Maybe our magic didn't work right, she realised.

Taranee turned to Will. "So, you think our friendship and our powers are connected?" she asked.

"Could be," Will said. Then she grimaced. "The only way to find out for sure is to go to Candracar. I'm sure the Oracle can explain everything. I just don't know how we're going to get there. We're powerless, and there are only three of us!"

Hay Lin felt disappointed all over again. Some team, she thought. Without more of W.I.T.C.H., we can't even walk on to the playing field, let alone get to Candracar.

But suddenly, she heard a voice at the gate call out, "Guess again!"

A head emerged from behind a stone pillar. It was Irma, throwing her arms open dramatically. "I'm here!" she announced with a flourish.

Hay Lin had never been so happy to see her friend.

I knew she'd come through! she thought. She just needed a little time. So now, we have almost everyone! W.I.T.C.H. minus one. This team has a shallow bench, but just enough players to cover the bases.

Smiling to herself, Hay Lin whispered, "Let the games begin!"

ELEVEN

Hidden deep inside the Temple of Candracar, Cornelia paced like a caged animal. Billowing clouds floated around her, glowing in pink and purple. At another time Cornelia would have found them beautiful – entrancing, even. But right now they looked about as appealing as bars across a window.

Luba's angry words kept echoing in Cornelia's mind: "Admit your guilt. Admit your guilt, and you will avoid being punished by the Council of Elders!"

But I'm not guilty of anything! Cornelia thought, bristling with anger. I was about to bring Caleb back when she got in my way! Luba did this, not me. I can't confess to a crime I didn't commit. I won't!

But it wasn't too hard for Cornelia to see the other side.

The Oracle is all-knowing, right? she wondered. Does that mean he'll know what I meant to do – or just what I did do? I meant to bring Caleb back. Instead, I brought back a Murmurer. The Murmurers were Phobos's eyes and ears, and Phobos was one of the greatest enemies Candracar has ever known. Will the Council listen to me? Will the Oracle understand?

Cornelia had a sinking feeling that she already knew the answer.

She glanced across the room at the place where Caleb lay and sighed. Nothing had worked out as she had hoped. Caleb was back – but not fully. He was a Murmurer – before he decided to take on human form; it was his strong will and convictions that had made him the leader of the rebels against Phobos.

Luba only let me bring him halfway back! she thought.

Caleb's eyes were open but unblinking, staring at the ceiling.

He was better off as a flower, Cornelia thought despondently. At least I could care for him then. Now they're going to take him to the dungeon!

Cornelia convulsed with sobs again, crouching in the mist so that Caleb couldn't see her. If he could see anything at all, he didn't need to see her lose it, Cornelia thought, wiping her eyes. If he was going to the dungeon, maybe she should have just confessed to anything Luba wanted. Maybe then she would have got to go, too. She would gladly have left everything else behind. Maybe it was the best she could hope for.

She thought back to the days she had spent in her apartment with only Caleb for company. Back when he was a flower, she recalled, she had sung to him. She had talked to him. She had acted as if he were real and could hear her. There was no reason not to speak to him now. She was not put off by his looks. No matter what Luba said, Cornelia knew her Caleb could not be a Murmurer at heart. He could not be evil – ever.

Drawing closer to his motionless body, she spoke very softly. "It shouldn't have ended like this!" she said as she sat beside him, feeling comforted once again by his presence.

The wave of comfort was followed by a rush of anger. "I just can't accept it! I don't want to!" she said, taking Caleb's face in her hands. She looked deep into his glassy eyes. "It was your willpower that made you who you were!" she said to him.

Lifting his head gently with her hands, she shook his head from side to side. But still she got no response. "Caleb!" she continued. "Caleb . . . you've got to listen to me! You've got to!"

She stroked his forehead. "You can't forget who you really are!" she cried. She picked up one of his limp hands and caressed his fingers lovingly. They felt so cold to the touch . . . so lifeless. "And you can't forget about us!"

She brought Caleb's hand to her lips and kissed it. She had vowed to be strong, for his sake. But it was so, so hard. . . . Her eyes overflowed, and her tears fell on Caleb's hand, which fit into hers as if the two were made for each other.

For a moment, the only sound in the room was that of Cornelia's gentle sobbing.

Then, suddenly, something happened.

Caleb the Murmurer sprang from the floor! He leaped into the air and drew his hand to his chest. "Your teardrop . . ." he roared.

He'd been launched like a rocket. Caleb flew toward the ceiling, arching backward, and as he came back down to the ground, he began to change.

His long hair began to morph into the familiar, floppy mop that Cornelia recognised so well.

His green skin slowly turned yellow, and then faded to white.

His glassy eyes were suddenly clear, blue, and focused. They gazed at Cornelia with a mixture of adoration and slight confusion.

And then he spoke, his voice low. "Your teardrop . . . within me . . . forever!"

He is back! Cornelia thought. The way he's meant to be! She rejoiced. She could hardly believe it. After all this time, her dreams were finally coming true!

She ran toward Caleb with her arms outstretched. It took her only a moment to reach him, and when she did, she wrapped her arms around his neck and squeezed as tightly as she could.

I will never let him go, she thought. Never ever. Not again.

"Caleb! It's really you!" she cried joyfully. There was nothing else to say. No words were enough to describe her relief . . . her bliss . . . her love. She thought that if she said anything else, the spell might be broken and he would disappear again.

"Cornelia!" Caleb cried, assuring her that he was definitely real.

They stood there, holding each other, for what seemed to each of them like weeks. Cornelia closed her eyes to take in the feeling of having Caleb back in her arms, to really live it. And when she peeked at him, from time to time, he was always looking back at her. He couldn't keep his eyes off her.

Caleb was the first to move.

Don't! Cornelia thought. It hasn't been long enough. He can't let me go yet.

But Caleb's embrace was not over, only shifting. Now his hands were around her waist, pulling her even closer.

"Finally," Cornelia whispered. Being close to Caleb felt like coming home. She finally felt at peace.

Caleb whirled her around. They danced through the hidden chamber, giddy with delight. Then Caleb grew serious. "I owe you my life!" he said sincerely.

Cornelia covered her eyes with her hands. She turned away from his heartfelt look. "Don't look at me!" she cried. "I've become a monster!"

Now that Caleb is back, I don't want to think of what I've done, she thought. I've stopped at nothing. I've misused my power – and I've alienated my friends.

"I know everything that happened to you," he said gently. "And you shouldn't worry – you're still beautiful! Even after Phobos struck me down," he continued to explain, "I never stopped hearing what was going on."

So Caleb doesn't care that my magic raged out of control? Cornelia wondered. He doesn't care that I imprisoned Luba or abandoned my friends?

"I heard you when you spoke to me," Caleb continued, "even if I couldn't answer you." Caleb stroked Cornelia's hair. "It was your voice that kept me from reverting completely!"

It was worth it, then, Cornelia thought. But how do you say, "You're welcome" for something so huge?

"I don't . . ." she stammered.

Caleb put his hand over her mouth to keep her from saying anything else. He drew her more closely to him and reassured her: "Don't worry!" he said.

But Cornelia was worried. Suddenly, the thought of all of her problems came flooding back into her brain: Luba. The Council. The dungeons.

"We have to escape!" she said to Caleb with alarm. "The Keeper of the Aurameres wants to . . ."

She'd forgotten that Caleb knew everything there was to know. He held her hands. He calmed her with his eyes. And he said exactly what Cornelia needed to hear.

"No, we're not going to run away," he declared. "We'll face Luba and the Council together!"

Cornelia despaired. "But how?" she cried. "I don't have any powers!"

There is nothing between us and the Council's verdict, she thought. Nothing between us and their everlasting punishment. I have no magic. And we have no friends to back us up.

"Don't say that!" Caleb warned her.

He drew Cornelia toward him, enfolding her in his arms, protecting her. And, as Cornelia raised her lips to his, Caleb explained why she had nothing to be afraid of. Hope was how he had survived. Hope was how he had managed to come back. Caleb knew it, and Cornelia knew it, too. She allowed herself a ray of hope. "Together we have the strongest power there is!" Caleb said.

And with a kiss he eased Cornelia's mind and heart.

TWELVE

Luba felt ready to retch as she quietly observed the Guardian and the Murmurer kissing and carrying on.

"It's preposterous!" she muttered. "Absolutely ridiculous!" Her jaw dropped open as she watched the two cling to each other, crying and declaring their love. "What makes that girl think she can conduct herself that way right here in Candracar? Does she not appreciate what we have done for her?"

Luba's whiskers quivered with anger. *So, it is not enough that she used her magic to introduce the enemy into our Temple and our world. Now she must go ahead and embrace him, too! Defy all that should be precious to her! Defy her destiny!*

Unable to bear it any longer, Luba tore herself away and prepared to meet the Council.

They sent me to Heatherfield to atone, she remembered, *and now I will report back to them. I may have erred in creating an Altermere. But they will find that the Guardian's error is far greater. Wait until they see what she has done with her powers. She has undermined the Council at every step of the way. She is the one who will need to atone now!*

When she thought of the scene that was playing itself out in the distant chamber, she smiled. *Perhaps the Council would like to watch a bit of this,* she thought. *I am sure they will find it most instructive.*

Once again, the Council of Elders sat in the ornate circular hall, lining several benches. Once again, the Oracle and Tibor, his trusted adviser, stared at Luba as she spoke to the gathering from the centre of the room.

Breathlessly, Luba explained all that had happened since the end of her trial: her attempt to warn the Guardian about her potent strength; the Guardian's flagrant disregard for her safety – and for the age-old rules of Candracar; the Guardian's vicious attack on her, a member of Candracar's Council.

"And now, this!" Luba exclaimed.

With a wave of her hand, she called forth the image of Cornelia and Caleb from inside the Temple. The image hovered in the air, light flickering all around it, illuminating the couple within and making it appear as though they were on a movie screen.

The chamber fell silent as the Council regarded the young lovers. Luba pretended to look at it, too, but she was really watching the Council members from the corner of her eye. Do they see the Guardian's weakness? she wondered. They must comprehend that everything the Guardian does is driven by emotion, by what she calls love! And where does this take their esteemed Guardian? Right into the arms of the enemy.

As the Council members began to shift in their seats, Luba readied her summation. She did not discuss what the Council members had just seen – the image, she concluded, spoke for itself.

"And now, may the Council decide," she

said grandly. "Have you finally understood?" Luba summoned up her strongest voice to make her final point. "She's brought back Phobos's servant!" she screeched. "You can see how dangerous she is!"

"That's funny," a voice drawled. "She looks more like she's in love to me. What's the problem with being in love, Luba?"

Leave it to Tibor, Luba seethed, to make light of this critical situation. His powers of perception are limited. He must not see the issues that are at stake.

For once, the Oracle seemed not to hear Tibor or take his words into account. "Have you managed to understand the Guardian's motives, Luba?" he asked gently.

He is listening, Luba thought. At last he sees the situation for what it is – out of control!

"Yes," she replied forcefully. "The Guardian has a rebellious temperament. I explained the situation to her, but she preferred to think only of herself. She has proven herself unworthy – as have all of her friends."

Luba saw a look of bewilderment pass over the face of a Council member, so she backtracked immediately. "But she, of course, is the worst of them all!" she assured the gathering.

Can't change the subject too quickly with this crowd, she noted. First things first – making the Guardians pay.

The Council of Elders erupted into argument. The chamber was soon filled with conversation, both angry and confused.

"This is unheard of!" one person shouted.

"Yet Candracar needs the five Guardians!" another voice argued.

Luba let the debate rage for some time. Dialogue is good, she thought. They are bound to come around and agree with me.

Eventually, however, she just had to step in. She was, after all, the one who had seen this treachery up close. She was the one with the solution.

"I call for Khandran!" she bellowed, silencing the room. "I'll call for sentencing of all the Guardians who have betrayed us – and for their replacement!"

Luba squinted at the gathered Council members. "These five Guardians were a terrible mistake!" she proclaimed. "I say we rid ourselves of them at once . . . and begin the search for the true Chosen Ones."

Luba stood back as the debate flared up again. She tried to stay patient and to keep her composure.

There need be no rush to judgment, she told herself, so long as they *do* judge the Guardians – in exactly the way I have called for!

THIRTEEN

Will sighed softly so that her friends couldn't hear. What happened to curling up on the couch and watching a movie with Mum, anyway? she wondered. She looked at her friends surrounding her. Everyone's waiting for me, she thought, and I don't know what to say!

The girls were standing in a town park not too far from Cornelia's apartment. The place was totally deserted. The only activity was pigeons poking through the trash. The only sound to be heard was the whoosh of the large fountain at the centre of the park.

I wish that I could leap in there right now, Will thought longingly. Have a swim and clear my head.

Instead, she had to come up with a way to

get to Candracar. To the very centre of infinity. No problem, right?

Without our powers, we're not going anywhere, Will thought.

She walked over to the fountain, avoiding her friends' eyes.

What happened? she wondered. I mean, how did we get here? One minute, we were fighting creatures in Metamoor and restoring the place to its rightful ruler. The next minute, we were barely speaking.

She looked pensively at her palm. Would she ever see the Heart of Candracar again? She ached to hold it again, to see the swirl of colours as her friends' powers came together. There had been nothing like it. When she had had the Heart, she always knew what to do. The Heart had helped her transform the girls' powers into potent magic. But the Heart had also transformed *her*. Without it she was weak. She was tongue-tied. She was just a new girl in town, trying to find her way.

We've been fighting so much, Will thought, that we've stopped talking. Did the other girls want their magic back, too? Will smiled to herself. It was the perfect time to ask them.

Taranee, Hay Lin, and Irma were milling around in the park silently. As Will approached Taranee, she looked at her expectantly. "So, what do you think we should do?" she asked.

Will took a deep breath. She hoped she wouldn't scare them off.

"Well, there are a couple of questions we should think over seriously," Will said.

Irma bounced over to where the two girls were standing. "As long as they're not too difficult," she joked.

"I'm not kidding!" Will retorted. "How often have we complained about what happened to us?"

Hay Lin seemed a little defensive. "Well . . . ok, so a couple of times we did! But that's not so serious, is it?" she asked.

No, no, thought Will. I don't think we're in trouble. I just want to know if you feel the way I do. She looked at the ground and fumbled for a response.

"Maybe it is serious," she said softly. Then she raised her head, eyes blazing. "We've got to figure out if we want our powers back – and most of all, why. Do you ever miss them? Do you feel different without them?"

For a moment, nobody said anything. They were confused, Will thought dejectedly. Well, she was, too.

Hay Lin drew her hands together and looked up at the stars. "I liked having powers, because we did important things. I was proud of what we did for Meridian."

Under the cover of darkness, Will beamed. She nodded to herself. Exactly!

Irma scrunched her face up. "I could tell you that it was nice having powers just to control quiz questions . . . but that might be a lie," she admitted.

Taranee's voice was low. It sounded as if she were trying not to cry. "Having powers made me braver!"

I'm gonna cry, too, if I'm not careful, Will realised. I guess I'm not alone! She looked around at her friends.

It was her turn to say something, and Will put it all on the line. If she couldn't tell her friends, she couldn't tell anybody. She couldn't look at any of them as she spoke. "Losing my powers was like losing a little part of myself," she confessed.

Hay Lin's eyes opened wide. "She's right!"

she announced. "It was like losing an important part of myself."

"Too important," Taranee whispered. "Like our friendship."

Suddenly something clicked in Will's mind. "And that's the next question," she said. "Do you think we're really friends?" She held her breath. She had been almost afraid to ask the question. She watched her friends' reactions.

"Of course we are!" Hay Lin exclaimed. "Why would you even ask that?"

"Because we stopped believing in us, Hay Lin," Will said. "We forgot something important, but the Heart of Candracar remembered. Friendship should never be neglected!"

Suddenly, Will had an idea.

She put her hand out, palm up. As if she knew just what Will wanted, Irma put her hand on top of Will's, the cuff of her orange jacket brushing against Will's hand. Soon, Hay Lin's thin and elegant hand was also on the pile. And then Taranee's.

At first the pile of hands just felt warm to Will. It felt cozy, caring. And then it started to feel a little different. She could feel something else happening . . . something magical. This friendship is the key to our powers, Will realised. She knew it before, but now she felt it in a different way. It was as absolute as gravity, as certain as the fact that spring followed winter. Together, we can do anything, Will breathed. Even reclaim our magic. Even reclaim the Heart.

The girls let their hands drop one by one.

"Together forever?" Taranee asked. Nobody had used those words, but that was what the hand thing was all about: jump-starting the friendship; jump-starting the magic.

"Of course!" Irma cried.

"That goes for those who are absent, too," Will added. "Cornelia is with us in spirit right now, even if her body isn't."

The thought of Cornelia stabbed Will's heart like a bolt of lightning. That was the point. They had to find her. In Candracar, they would learn how.

Suddenly Will's palm felt tingly. It was the afterglow left by her friends' hands – and also more. With no warning at all, something popped out of Will's palm: the Heart of Candracar! Because we are united! Will rejoiced. I will never again let it go.

The Heart was as beautiful as ever. The pink orb gleamed within the silver clasp that encircled it. It hovered above Will's palm, and Will spoke to it as if it were an old friend: "Heart of Candracar, are you listening? Take us to the Oracle!"

Her friends drew closer around the Heart, waiting for it to shoot out glistening teardrops of magic to each of them. A moment passed. But nothing happened.

"Feel anything?" Taranee asked nervously.

Will hated to admit it, but she didn't feel the familiar glow and rush of energy transforming her into her Guardian self.

"Nope. Only coldness," she said.

Hay Lin seemed not to feel the sense of gloom that had descended over Will and the others.

"So?" Hay Lin said. "Let's try again. We just have to believe more in *us*."

Irma huddled in closer to Hay Lin. "We just have to believe we're strong," she added.

"And something will happen!" Taranee chimed in.

Will extended her hand again and looked into Hay Lin's eyes, then Irma's and Taranee's in turn. She watched her friends, her true friends, as they stood there, believing in the power of the friendship.

We'll do this for as long as we have to, until we reach Candracar, Will thought. We have to believe.

FOURTEEN

Irma blinked. The light was so bright that she was temporarily blinded.

This feels like leaving a movie theatre on a sunny day, she thought. Times a million. What happened? Where are we?

She was desperate to find out. But she couldn't open her eyes.

Next thing she knew, Will was shouting, "We did it!"

"I knew it! I knew it! I knew it!" Hay Lin chanted.

I don't care if my eyeballs are singed forever, Irma decided. I *have* to open my eyes and see what is going on.

What she saw was beyond her wildest dreams. It was a sight that made her clap her hands in joy and smile like a fool.

They had made it to Candracar!

The bright light was intense, as the Temple was carved from iridescent crystal and stone, and the reflections were very strong.

And, as if that weren't enough, Irma looked down and got some more good news. We've transformed! she realised with shock. Like we always do when we unite through the Heart.

And not a minute too soon. She had missed this rockin' outfit!

For the first time in a long time, she was feeling pretty good.

Irma was now dressed in a flirty purple skirt over brilliantly coloured striped leggings. Her top was a deep shade of aqua that matched her eyes – and showed just enough of her shoulders. Too bad she couldn't wear those clothes to school, she thought.

Will, Taranee, and Hay Lin had been transformed, too, and they were every bit as excited as Irma was. It had been way too long since they had felt this way.

"The power of air is mine again!" Hay Lin sang as she floated around in a crazy, jubilant trance.

"The power of fire is in me!" Taranee said with wonder. She was mesmerised by a flame that had appeared in her hand, burning fiercely but not hurting anybody. Its light flickered and illuminated the joy on Taranee's face.

Suddenly, a stream of water began snaking around Irma's shoulder. It didn't spill onto the floor, because Irma had the water under control – her reflexes kicked in just as fast as they always had. Irma trailed her fingers through the cool water and seemed to feel refreshed from head to toe. *"Yesss!"* she cried.

She tore her eyes off her own personal river for just long enough to notice Hay Lin's grandmother smiling at them. She had been so caught up in playing with her newfound power she had been oblivious to her surroundings – until now. Yan Lin was sitting in the centre of the circular room the girls had arrived in, right next to the Oracle and the Elder with the long white beard that swept the floor.

"Welcome back to Candracar, girls," Yan Lin said warmly, her eyes crinkling as she broke into a huge smile. As always, the voice was warm and comforting, putting the young Guardians instantly at ease.

Irma was loving having her powers back. She basked in Yan Lin's good vibe and in the wise presence of the Oracle. And then she noticed that something else was going on.

There were other people there, too, Irma thought. Or *creatures* – whatever you call those who make up the Council of Elders.

They were sitting on benches lining the room. Irma could hear a voice rising and falling and she realised suddenly why everyone had gathered. They were there listening to some-body speak.

Another meeting! Irma almost giggled out loud. Like the Happy Bears, all over again! Maybe they, too, were playing some kind of game.

The speaker was scowling and flailing her arms all about. Then she pointed an accusa-tory finger at the Oracle. "Declare Khandran, Oracle!" she demanded. "Now!"

What's her problem? Irma wondered. What is she talking about?

The Oracle tried to stop her. "Luba . . ." he said loudly.

Irma didn't recognise that name, but she recognised who the Oracle was talking to.

Uh-oh, she thought. That's the cat-woman who disappeared with Cornelia. Didn't Taranee mention something earlier about the judgment of the Council? Could this be a court or trial of some kind?

Irma had no idea what was happening . . . and she didn't like that at all.

Then a bearded Elder spoke up and Irma's musings were interrupted. "Look!" the creature cried, pointing at Irma and her friends.

Luba's head swiveled in their direction, and she saw the girls for the first time. "How have they got their powers back?" she yowled at the top of her lungs.

It wasn't easy, Irma thought. We should get some extra credit for this – it was hard work getting here.

Will chose that moment to approach the Oracle. "Oracle, we need to speak with you!" she pleaded.

He nodded knowingly. "I know why you have come," he answered.

"Of course! To stand trial!" Luba roared, interrupting him.

I don't think so, Irma thought. Why would we stand trial? Let the Oracle talk already!

Luba walked toward the girls and glowered at them. "I don't know how you got here," she shouted, "but that doesn't change our laws!" Then she addressed the Oracle. "In undergoing Khandran," she explained, "they will have the chance to defend themselves. Even if what they have done is inexcusable."

Hay Lin looked terrified. "Grandma!" she cried, edging toward Yan Lin as if for protection from this beast.

But Irma was totally confused. "I must have missed a few episodes," she whispered to Will. "What's the lynx-face blabbering about?"

Defend ourselves against what? she added silently to herself when Will didn't respond. This doesn't make any sense.

Suddenly she had the sense that they'd walked into a courtroom – and that they were about to be convicted. The happiness she'd felt a few moments ago melted away.

Will was pale and still. She looked as if she were about to faint.

The spectators on the benches began to mumble. The noise grew louder and more insistent until the Oracle raised his hand.

"Enough," he commanded.

He didn't raise his voice, Irma noticed. But everyone did his bidding.

"It is time for harmony to return to this place," he said.

The Oracle looked at each of the girls, one by one. Then he homed right in on Luba.

"These girls travelled here by rediscovering the power of their friendship and, with it, their powers!" he exclaimed. He raised his hand again, as if to silence anyone who dared object to what he was saying. "By doing this," he continued, "they have proved that they are worthy of their role."

Irma felt a little surge of pride well up in her chest. He knows what we went through, she thought. He appreciates how hard this was for us.

"Therefore," the Oracle said, "I will not declare Khandran. For them, no trial is needed!"

So, we're off the hook? Irma wondered.

Taranee caught her eye and gave her a thumbs-up. Hay Lin grinned at her grandmother.

Irma took a long deep breath. "I have the impression we just got out of something really bad," she whispered to Will.

But the Oracle wasn't finished. Slowly, he walked toward the crowd that was gathered on the benches. "Those of you convinced of the contrary, speak now."

Nobody uttered a word till a being with two antennae stood up. "The Council upholds your decision, Oracle," he said, pulling at his beard.

Irma was so busy marvelling at the collection of strange characters on the benches that she almost missed what the creature said next.

"But the fifth Guardian is a different matter," he said.

Fifth Guardian? Irma thought. Math wasn't her strong suit, but even she knew there were only four Guardians in the room. Was he talking about Cornelia? What had she done? She wasn't even there to stand up for herself. How was that fair?

Luba cackled and marched toward the Council. "The fifth Guardian still hasn't regained her powers," she informed the Council members with a note of triumph in her voice. "Her Auramere is still silent! Therefore, her offence must be punished!" She raised her fist in the air and shook it.

"What offence?" muttered Will.

Irma looked at Will and then back at Luba. Clearly, this trial was not over. While the four of them seemed to be off the hook, Cornelia was still in major trouble.

Friends stick together, Irma vowed. If only she knew where Cornelia was, so that she could help her. It seemed that Cornelia more than any of them really needed the power of friendship at that moment. She just hoped it wasn't too late.

FIFTEEN

So this is it, Cornelia shivered. The moment of judgment is at hand.

She walked bravely toward the majestic hall, her gaze fixed squarely ahead of her. She dared not look at the imposing structure around her – the intricate carvings on the walls, the massive windows, the beautiful sculptures.

Once, she remembered, I thought Candracar was the most peaceful and tranquil place. Now, I don't know what's what anymore. Does this place have a dungeon? Does the Council of Elders here in Candracar have trials . . . and punishments?

Cornelia squeezed her eyes shut so she wouldn't start crying again. This was the end of her life as a

Guardian. It was the end of her life as she knew it, period. Luba was out for revenge.

The only saving grace was Caleb. He stood next to her and patted her hand as they approached the massive, arched doorway. Beams of light shone through windows high above.

My knight in shining armor, Cornelia thought. Even if he's not on horseback. Even if he's only in a tattered cloak. He is the only reason I can face the Council. He is the only hope I have.

The pair crossed the threshold humbly and quietly, but their peace was quickly shattered. They were greeted with an angry catcall.

I should have guessed we couldn't enter undetected, Cornelia thought resentfully. She's been waiting for us.

The "she" Cornelia referred to was Luba – who now stood in the centre of a large room, an intense expression on her face.

"Look!" shrieked Luba. "Before your very eyes!"

Cornelia gazed at the ground, allowing Caleb to guide her by the elbow.

Just put one foot in front of the other, she

thought. That's all you have to do.

Then, in her mind, something snapped.

I will not let the Council see me cower! she decided. I didn't do anything wrong. They must see me strong and proud.

Cornelia defiantly shook her long blonde hair and lifted her chin as she surveyed the room. She saw the circular chamber in which the Council members buzzed with anticipation. She saw the curious glances thrown her way by some of the members. She saw the Oracle seated between Tibor and Yan Lin.

But she also saw something that made her do a double take. She let out a little gasp and squeezed Caleb's hand. Will, Irma, Taranee, and Hay Lin were standing there – fully transformed! Her friends. Right there in Candracar, just when she needed them the most.

Taranee and Irma faced her with surprised looks on their faces.

"Caleb?" Taranee asked under her breath.

Cornelia could hear Irma answering. "Man, I shouldn't say it," she whispered, "but sometimes that girl is a real legend!"

It took all of Cornelia's self-control not to react. Was she allowed to talk to them? She didn't want to do anything to hurt her case.

But then the girls were storming her, crowding around her.

Will was the first, of course. "Cornelia!" she cried. "Are you all right?"

"How did you manage?" Hay Lin asked.

"I'm not really sure myself," Cornelia stammered. "I thought I'd never see you all again!" she whispered.

I should have known better, Cornelia thought with a great sense of relief. We are bonded forever, wherever we are.

"I'm so happy to see you guys!" she sputtered lamely. "How did you get here? How did you know?" Cornelia was flooded with questions she wanted to ask and then with a sudden sense of calm.

While she was reunited with her friends, Caleb sauntered up to the Oracle. "May I have the chance to speak?" he asked.

"Stop, Murmurer!" Luba cried. She blocked his way, as if he presented a grave danger to the Oracle. She glared at him as she said, "Don't you dare go near the lord of Candracar!"

Caleb extended both of his hands, palms out, as if to surrender. "Don't call me

Murmurer," he said politely. "My name is Caleb."

Luba gaped. She was ready to explode – but then the Oracle stepped in, and Luba pressed her lips together in a visible effort to restrain herself. Her whiskers twitched, and her hands balled up, but she remained silent.

"Let him pass," the Oracle ordered her. "You know perfectly well he can do nothing to hurt us." He turned his attention to Caleb, and in his calm, rational voice addressed the young man. "Speak freely, Caleb. The Council is listening."

Cornelia held her breath. She didn't know what Caleb would say. What *could* he say?

"If Cornelia made a mistake," Caleb began, "it was all my fault. And that is why I ask that she be given her power back."

Cornelia tried to hold herself together. It was not his fault! she wanted to scream. I did this all by myself! I brought him back, because I loved him and couldn't live without him!

Suddenly, Caleb had some backup.

"We ask for the same. Please restore her power," Taranee said firmly, her gaze shifting between Cornelia and the Oracle.

"We've always been a team, and we want to keep being one," Hay Lin added, looking hurt, but stubborn.

Cornelia couldn't help glancing over to see Yan Lin's reaction.

Sure enough, the elderly Guardian was silently mouthing some words to Tibor: *Now, that's my granddaughter.*

She's proud of Hay Lin, Cornelia thought. And so am I.

A warm feeling washed over her. No matter what happened, she would never forget the way her friends were there for her at that moment.

But before Cornelia's happiness could take hold, Luba was back. She lunged toward Caleb and hissed at the Oracle. "Don't listen to him! That being is Phobos's creation! He is danger-ous!"

"So, punish me, not Cornelia!" Caleb re-torted.

Cornelia froze. No! she thought, frowning. Don't punish *anybody* on these trumped-up charges!

This was not supposed to be happening. Caleb didn't know what he was doing! But

Cornelia realised he did know – he was sacrificing himself so that her powers would be preserved.

"I can give her back her power," Caleb explained, "the power she used to bring me back. And, in exchange – if the Council will allow me to do so – I will remain in the Temple as your servant."

A servant? Cornelia bristled. I want him to stay with me, she thought

Trying not to panic, she waited to see what happened. Would anybody in Candracar go for this?

The Oracle closed his eyes. He hummed and swayed from side to side, deep in meditation. At last he nodded.

Cornelia shivered.

Then a Council member stood up to speak. The antennae on his head bobbled as he said, "The Council has observed and understood. It is willing to accept Caleb's offer."

Cornelia's heart was in her throat. This isn't what I wanted, she despaired. Caleb and I will be forced apart again!

"Therefore, proceed," the Oracle intoned, with a mighty strength. "May the power of the earth be returned to its legitimate bearer!"

Cornelia was hardly thinking about the power she had gained. She was thinking only about what she had just lost.

Her friends, however, were jumping and screaming for joy. Their happy voices registered in the back of Cornelia's mind.

"Wow! Together again!" Hay Lin cheered.

"And we'll never split up, ever again!" Will yelled.

It's true, Cornelia thought. *We* won't split up. But Caleb and I *will* be separated! I can't believe this is happening all over again.

Caleb approached her, his eyes shining with unshed tears.

He doesn't want this, either, Cornelia thought. But he thinks it is the only way. I want to throw my arms around him! I want to kiss him a thousand times!

But even she knew that that was impossible in the Council hall. Their goodbye would have to be more discreet than that.

Caleb waved awkwardly to Cornelia and backed away. She had to touch him, at least, she thought. After all he had done, and in case she never saw him again! She reached for his hand and grabbed it with all the force she had. He knew how she felt, she assured herself. Even if she could not say it just then.

He wrapped his hand lovingly around hers. His eyes said, *I will be back!* Cornelia reached to touch his shoulder one last time.

Holding Caleb's hand, Cornelia looked over at her friends. They were beaming at her. And for the first time in a very long time, Cornelia felt at peace. The situation was far from perfect, but at that moment she had Caleb and her friends at her side. She felt a surge of bravery well up inside of her. There was nothing that she couldn't face now.